OCEANS
APART

JERRY BAGGETT

Artwork by Chuck Estvan

ISBN 978-1-64003-020-6 (Paperback)
ISBN 978-1-64003-021-3 (Digital)

Covenant Books, Inc.
11661 Hwy 707
Murrells Inlet, SC 29576
www.covenantbooks.com

CONTENTS

ACKNOWLEDGEMENT

To Digby, Bob, and Johnny Our brothers, our heroes and the loving families they left behind.

A special thanks to Toni Lopopolo for her important advice on Voice and charged Dialog.

And my heart-felt appreciation to my brother Phil and wife Vicki for patiently assisting me in understanding the mysteries of the modern computer.

CHAPTER 1

Guadalupe Island, Mexico

June 15, 2015

The atmosphere close to the island was oppressive. Mike fileted the fleshy body and tossed the skeleton overboard—their meal for this evening. Not even a light breeze, he hated damn sweat rolling down his back.

"You know, Joel, I'm concerned. We left Cabo so fast after we kicked hell out of that narco shit. Need some knowledge of what's going on. It's possible they picked up our trail. He's not likely to take a beating and just forget about it."

Joel took the pressure regulator off a dive tank and dropped it in fresh water. "Diverting to Guadalupe Island bought us a few days. We've had fun, but it's probably time to move our asses."

"Yeah, you haven't spotted that big sport fisher again that passed south of us a few days ago?"

Joel shook his head. "The more reason to grab the hook and get the hell out of Mexico. Those guys avoided close contact with us for a reason."

"I agree. It's better to be safe than sorry. The weather report looks decent for the next few days, Joel. Let's plan on getting underway before dawn."

"Sound's good, we'll buck a fifteen-knot headwind after a couple hundred miles out. Already stayed late in the season for these waters."

"More than likely," Mike said, "I'm glad we made the trip out here. Always wanted to dive Guadalupe Island. Never seen so damn many sea bass that big anywhere. Also, some good-sized lobsters poking their heads outa every crevice around Adventro rock."

"Don't forget about all the big sheepshead in that big cove. Pomene cove, wasn't it? Gonna run outa freezer space if we stay around here any longer."

"Let's get the phone calls to the LA office out of the way, Joel. Those guys hate ringing cell phones after working hours."

～～～

The bright morning sun forced Mike to turn his head toward the long straight wake of *Blue Dolphin*, a school of porpoise playing in the wake. He admired the activity. Something else caught his eye. He picked up the field glasses for a better look. A sea lion. Whoa! Wait a minute. Looks like a body hung up on kelp. He turned off the autopilot and pulled back on the throttles. "Joel, get your butt up here."

Joel brought in a tray from the galley, bear claws, and a decanter of hot coffee. "What's up?"

"Take the helm! Looks like a body hung up on the kelp, off to port, toward the island. Ease us close for a better look. I'm going down. Take it slow. Get the swim platform near as possible without disturbing anything."

"Yell out if you need me. The hailer will pick up your voice."

Close up, Mike saw a body. A woman. Alive. She held out her hands, wrists bound, fought to keep her face above water. Mike dove in, got his arm around her neck, face up,

10

kicked his way to the swim platform, and pushed her up on the deck.

"Joel, give me a hand. Hurry, Joel."

CHAPTER 2

Tuscaloosa, Alabama

December 2005

Mike McGowin slid his feet off the coffee table, stretched, took the cold beer from Bill Campbell. He loved the violence of big-time college football, proud of his own aggressive reputation. "Hey, pal, we partying tonight?"

Bill nodded. "So, Mike, no more Bama football, no more painkillers, no more wind sprints and two-a-day practice sessions. The US Army might have you longing to be back in the game."

"Nah, Bill! Been there, done that, enjoyed every minute. I'm anxious to take a new direction. Got a lot of catching up to do."

"Yeah! Let's go get cleaned up. Can't keep the ladies waiting." He looked at Mike with a grin, "You behave yourself around my favorite girl tonight. Someday you have to give me your secret for charming the beauties."

"Come on, Bill, you do all right. I'm really gon'o miss you. Best roommate ever."

"You haven't packed away your dinner jacket, have you? In all that stuff you've stored away in your closets?"

"I pulled it out and cleaned it up after your invite. It's a good thing my mom shipped me off with a full wardrobe. I've never unpacked most of that crap. I told her Bama football didn't leave time for many outside activities. She's the reason we share this apartment, as you know. I think she realized it'd take a big place to store all this useless stuff. A quiet place to study was secondary to her. Was a party girl in her college days."

Mike's dressed in a dark dinner jacket with a pleated shirt, white gold, and black studs, matching cuff links and light-gray slacks. Damn! He looked good.

"Hey, Bill. You ready? I am. Do I have to wear the bow-tie if I'm not going to the ball?"

"Open collar with dinner jacket's okay for the cocktail party. Son of a gun, Mike, for a big bad ass, you clean up nice. I may have to change my mind about letting you meet Casey."

Mike studied his pal. Bill had no idea how good he looked. Damn good friend too. "Do you suppose we can walk the three blocks to the Phi Kappa Sigma house without freezing our asses off? I could really use the exercise."

"Feel free to walk, big guy. I need my car. I'm taking Casey straight to the ballroom after the cocktail party."

Mike had an easy jog to the frat house and found Bill talking to friends inside the front door. He led Mike to the coat check girl, who said, "Hi, handsome," and tossed the coat onto a full table.

He looked around and was impressed. A large white Christmas tree, then a brightly decorated main dining room and roaring fire in a stone fireplace. Smartly dressed servers passed through the crowd with trays of glistening champagne and delicious-looking hors d'oeuvres.

Bill drifted into the crowd and greeted friends and fraternity brothers.

A head taller than anyone else, Mike looked out over the sea of happy people and enjoyed the mixture of Christmas carols and easy-listening jazz heard above the laughter and tinkling of glasses. He sipped his second glass of champagne and looked at a tall dark-haired girl holding a champagne glass, talking to a man near the fireplace. Her deep-throated laugh stimulated his interest. He headed in her direction until someone grabbed his shoulder.

"Mike, I thought you accepted that Forty-Niner offer and bailed."

"No, Charley, that was a decent offer but not in my plans for the future."

"I read you're not entering the draft, but I don't believe it."

"Yeah, I have a couple of years obligated to Uncle Sam before making permanent plans. Say, Charley, who's that tall brunette with the long legs standing near the Christmas tree?"

"I don't know, Mike. She's certainly attractive, with a Delta Zeta pin on that beautiful chest. Someone said she's from Las Vegas, maybe a showgirl."

"Shit, Charley, I think I'm falling in love. Maybe I've been living with the animals too long. You don't suppose I'll have to kill her friend if I mosey over and talk to her, do you?"

Charley laughed. "Nah, don't rush it. You'll know everybody here within an hour."

CHAPTER 3

Tracy Conwell

December 2005

Tracy Conwell looked around, accepted a glass of bubbly, and admired the well-dressed group of people. A whole week here with Cathy, she couldn't wait. Last week had been hard. Hell, all last month was hard. The last game against sister program Nevada, horrible, lost big. She wanted some excitement. She moved around near the big fireplace, enjoying talking sports with several interesting men. Ben started talking about legal briefs. Boring. She saw Cathy waving her over. She said, "Excuse me, Ben," and weaved her way through the crowd, stopping near Cathy.

Cathy grabbed her hand. "Mike, I want you to meet my cousin Tracy. She's a jock like you, only prettier. Anyway, we grew up together in Las Vegas. He's a cocky bastard, Tracy, but lovable when on good behavior." She looked hard at Mike. "Don't let his schoolboy charm get you. Mike, you look after Tracy. Ben and I are leaving early for the formal dance at the Hilton."

Tracy was curious about this guy. She'd caught him looking a few times. Too good-looking, probably all into himself. "So, Mike, I've never been to a formal affair like this before. Is it a usual thing here?"

"Most of the Greek clubs have at least one formal cocktail party, followed by a formal dance at one of the hotel ballrooms. Usually held during the fall semester, around the holidays."

15

She swallowed the last of the bubbly. "Well! How long have you known Cathy?"

He looked at her. "We were pretty close our sophomore year. She claimed I only wanted help with my chemistry class."

Mike grabbed a couple glasses of champagne from a passing server and passed one to Tracy.

She said, "You look like you might play basketball."

"No, but I'm pretty good at pocket pool, and sometimes I win at dodgeball."

"Now I know who you are. Mike McGowin, the bone-breaking linebacker all the pro teams are talking about. You're holding out for more money."

"Not for more money. I made a firm commitment to the Army. Then there's the family corporation."

I read the sports pages. What's up with this guy?

She touched his arm, feeling a bit reckless. "I can't imagine a guy your age turning down a multimillion-dollar contract. Was it because Daddy said come home?"

"I loved playing football at Alabama, but I'm anxious to be more productive. After the Army, I want to build things with my hands and mind."

Tracy's antenna quivered. *Is this guy for real?*

She touched Mike's arm again. "Let's move farther away from the fire." They stopped near the over-decorated Christmas tree. They talked about other athletes and a few mutual friends. She sensed he was trying to behave, not too forward. He held her arm when they moved around and made eye contact, definitely interested.

Tracy said, "Mike, you're not with someone, are you?"

Mike smiled and shook his head.

Tracy added, "I'm not used to drinking. Would I be too forward by suggesting a bite to eat somewhere the music isn't too loud? This fine champagne could upset the apple cart if I'm not careful."

"No, I would be delighted. I know just the place. I'll let Cathy know. She must have her cell phone."

Tracy thought, *So easy to fall for this big guy, seems interested in everything about me.* He just wants to score.

Bill Campbell returned with his friend and introduced himself to Tracy. "And this is my friend Casey."

Casey immediately turned to Mike. "And you must be Mike, the roommate that's never there. Bill has spoken so highly of you."

Tracy turned awkwardly to avoid Mike's foot and lost her balance, causing both to fall toward the brightly lit Christmas tree. Barely avoided a catastrophe. Damn champagne.

Mike quickly pulled her in tight against his chest and turned to fall with his back to the floor. After a moment, he gently placed a hand to each side of Tracy's face and tenderly kissed her soft lips.

Standing nearby, Casey said, "Oh my god, Tracy! Are you hurt?"

Bill quickly reached down and pulled Tracy to her feet.

On unsteady legs, she said, "No, I'm not hurt, just embarrassed and a little damp." She laughed, set the tone for those gathered around. "I'm fine. I was careless."

Mike said, "Should I wait for you here while you're in the ladies' room? I'll drive you for a change of clothes."

"That would be nice. I won't be long." It could've been the champagne.

Bill said, "The wine spilled down the front of her beautiful cocktail dress. She sure handles it well."

Tracy walked toward Mike, smiling at their predicament. "Let's grab our coats and go for dry clothes."

"Wait! I almost forgot. My car's at the apartment. I can hoof it over and be back in a few minutes."

"Frankly, I think the walk would be great if it's not too far. My coat will be warm enough for me." She hoped her A personality wouldn't get her in trouble.

At the door, Tracy said, "Lucky dog. How the hell did a jock on an athletic scholarship manage a place like this?"

"To be honest, this place was arranged by my crazy mother through my father's alumni association. The deal was made well in advance of my showing up on campus. I prefer not to get into it right now if you don't mind, but I know what you were thinking."

"What was I thinking?"

"That this pad's for wild parties. Football players at Alabama don't have time for that if they also want a decent education. I loved playing football, spent most of my time with teammates and coaching staff at the dorm. But there were periods when I needed quiet study time. Then this place was a blessing."

"I didn't mean it like it sounded. I know how hard you worked to be good at football. I'm just jealous, believe me. I worked my ass off at UNLV too, as a basketball player on scholarship struggling to keep at least a 3.0 GPA. I'll be twenty-one next month, and I still live at home. So don't let my crankiness get to you. This is my Christmas vacation, and I've enjoyed your company very much."

She knew he liked looking at her in the wet clothes.

"I have an assortment of sweats and stuff if you want to try something like that. We can go casual some place."

Tracy noticed the neatly made king-size bed. She moved past two bare bureaus and stopped at the double closets. She moved from one closet to the other, fascinated. One was full of casual shirts and other attire. The other, crowded with luggage, opened-on luggage stands, some, tightly packed as if ready for a long trip.

"Where does your girlfriend keep her belongings?"

"I told you. There hasn't been time for girlfriends or serious involvements in my life. Sure, I've had very casual involvements, but no one special."

"I know. I'm only pulling your chain some." She looked at the open drawers he'd pulled out. "May I look those over?" She pulled out several sets of sweats, spreading them on the bed.

Mike broke her concentration. "I'm going to need a pair of those for myself. I can't go dressed like this while the most beautiful girl in the world goes on the town modeling men's athletic wear."

Tracy tried on several pairs of sweats. She still looked feminine enough. She pulled her long dark hair back, forming a ponytail. She secured it in place with a sweatband normally worn on the wrist. She left the pearl necklace on a bureau top. *I can't believe I'm doing this.*

She rejoined Mike. "Are you sure you don't have ladies' underwear around here someplace?"

"Wow, I can't believe what you did to my sweats! Uh-oh, no shoes. I'll check Bill's closet." He returned moments later with a pair of low-cut canvass deck shoes and a new pair of athletic socks. "Here, try these on while I get out of this wet shirt."

She watched Mike strip off the soiled shirt until he turned, nodded, and closed the bedroom door, still fascinated by the wide shoulders and highly defined back muscles. She tried on the shoes. To her surprise, nearly a perfect fit. For once, big feet are good. *After all, I'm five feet nine inches tall. That's as tall as some men I know.*

Mike left his bedroom dressed similar to Tracy: running shoes, sweat pants, and a plain navy-colored sweat shirt. "Okay! Let's go fill that gorgeous body with some comfort food."

"Mike, you were a Bama athlete! Don't you want to wear the Bama colors? You have several nice workout suits in the bedroom."

"No. Not now," he said. "I'm a soon-to-be-forgotten college athlete and prefer to look ahead toward the future, not behind. Maybe it's a dread of the unknown. I don't know why I feel that way. It just seems less important to me now."

She watched him walk to the closet and select two hooded jackets and toss one to her.

"Hey! I know a place for a good late-night steak. How does that sound?"

He opened the passenger door of a five-year-old BMW sedan, one hand on Tracy's elbow.

"Gee, Mike, you're a constant surprise." Twenty minutes later, they pulled off the two-lane highway. "Roadhouse," Tracy said, reading the bright sign over a large log structure placed back beneath huge pine trees. There were half a dozen cars and several pickup trucks, most parked in front of the brightly decorated restaurant.

Mike opened a heavy wooden door. They passed through a small mudroom and into a warm, well-decorated dining room. The dance floor was surrounded by padded oval-shaped booths across from a well-stocked bar.

She looked around and hesitated. "Look, another beautiful Christmas tree for us to fall into."

Mike laughed. "You know darn well that fall was contrived just so I could pull you close and kiss you."

"You're impressed with yourself, aren't you, Mr. Linebacker? That kiss did seem kind of special." *Why did I say that? Can't let him know.*

Mike reached out and touched her hand lightly. "Someday you're going to be the mother of my children. You know that, don't you?"

"Like hell I am. Arrogance gets you nowhere. Maybe that kiss wasn't so special."

"Saved by the bell," Mike said as an attractive older woman stepped up to take their order.

"What would you folks like to drink?"

Mike looked at Tracy. "Does a glass of Syrah sound okay to you, or would you like something different?"

"That would be nice as long as we order soon." *Be careful now, one more might be over the edge.*

He looked at the waitress. "Give us a bottle of your best Syrah, and let us look over a menu as soon as possible. This poor waif has been wandering the hinterlands without proper nourishment."

She glared at Mike. "You! Smart-ass. All the way here your stomach made noises like my old Volkswagen climbing a hill." *He just ordered a bottle, not a glass. I'm okay I think.*

Returning with the wine, the friendly waitress said, "The filet mignon is particularly good this evening, as well as the New York."

Tracy spoke first. "The filet sounds good to me, with all the trimmings. Mike? Medium rare?"

"Medium rare, but I'll have the New York the same way with all the trimmings."

Throughout the meal, she thought of that tender kiss; she asked more personal questions. They were answered; she became more aware of his tenderness. *Why can't I meet this most perfect man on my own home base? I'm not interested in a short-term romance.*

She said, "Dance with me, Mike!" He led her onto the dance floor.

"It must be the music. I've never felt so mellow. The soft tunes are wonderful." She placed one hand on his shoulder and gently toyed with the hair at his neckline. Soon other couples joined them on the floor.

"I'm enjoying myself immensely. You must have concerns about me, a strange girl in a strange town, with a strange man."

"No! I believe we all have dreams where suddenly that special person appears out of nowhere and fulfills that dream. I certainly think about it, and you are the most attractive and interesting woman I have ever known."

"It just hasn't happened with me. Am I only imagining that those things happen to people like me?"

"I see you as patiently preparing yourself for all kinds of opportunities yet to come."

How in hell did he pick up on that?

They spent more and more time on the dance floor, enjoying the closeness in each other's arms. The wine bottles were empty, the dining room closed, and the band packed up to go home. *What am I doing? I've never been this forward in all my life.*

"Mike, the music has stopped. Shouldn't we leave the dance floor?"

He lifted her face tenderly and looked into her beautiful green eyes. "We can't allow this evening to end so soon. I've finally found someone I can care for. Where in the world have you been hiding all my life?"

"I don't know, Mike. I'm afraid that kiss meant much more than I wish to admit. I've never had this problem before." *This better be a dream.*

On the drive back to his apartment, Tracy said, "I don't know what to do. I'm not prepared to stay overnight. I want very much to be with you, but what should I do?" I know what I should do. I'm old enough to know better, but maybe too young to resist this guy.

Mike removed his hand from Tracy's knee, rubbing it over the five-o'clock shadow now evident on his face. "You must see Cathy tomorrow for sure. Are you willing to rough it with me until then? Your beautiful cocktail dress will be dry. Or we can get you some casual clothes as soon as the stores open. I can afford it."

She was impressed with his warmth and sincerity. Different from anyone she had ever known.

Mike said, "Let's do this. Tomorrow morning, at a decent hour, call Cathy and let her know that we're shopping. And tell her what your plans are beyond that."

"I think that might work. Are you sure about shopping on my behalf? Please don't make me feel like I traded a bit of myself for a few items of clothing. This is all new to me. I'm very unsure of myself right now." *I hope like hell I'm doing the right thing.*

Back at Mike's apartment, Tracy said, "I'm not accustomed to sleeping bare. Do you mind if I snoop around in your stuff a little more?" Moments later she held up a large short-sleeved T-shirt with USC printed on the back. "Ha, you traitor! Look what you were hiding."

Mike smiled. "I once thought that might be my team. I visited Alabama and was sold on the sincerity, dedication to football, and friendliness of everyone I met."

Mike barely touched her lips with his. She responded with the tip of her tongue. They explored each other's body. Soon passionate kissing chafed Tracy's face. She was beyond caring. Their tongues touched and tangled lightly at first, then moved furiously as Mike held one breast, then the other. Tracy reacted with a soft intake of breath, relaxed, and let him know that everything was going well.

"Now, Mike. Show me now, please."

Mike hesitated, realizing Tracy was a virgin. He forced himself to remain still for a moment and removed his lips from Tracy's. "You're still a virgin, Tracy. Why didn't you tell me?"

"Would it make a difference, Mike? Please go ahead. I want you so much!"

Later, she was aware of the closeness, not moving. The warm, tender feeling she had for him had grown into a white hot emotional flame. She didn't know what to make of it all. She wiped a single tear from her cheek.

Mike was quiet. He placed his lips on her forehead. "I'm very much afraid. You've grown far too important to me, Tracy. My life's course has been charted across the world, and you'll be so far away."

"Yes, I know. We're going to be very special to each other, but it looks like life may get in the way."

CHAPTER 4

Los Angeles, California

May 2015

Mike McGowin looked down Santa Monica Boulevard from his fifth-floor office, wondering what afternoon traffic on coast highway would be like. He turned away from the window, stretched, and turned to relieve the pain in his back. An hour on the board with a run on the beach would be nice this evening.

The day started early at a Van Nuys construction site. He'd confronted a combative general contractor who had insisted on cutting corners at their new fifty-thousand-square-foot low-rise office complex. The shoddy work gained the attention of the anchor tenant. Not acceptable. Mike issued a last warning.

"No more deviations from the contract, Halloran. Core samples prove you poured the most recent ten thousand square feet of ground-level flooring with less than first-grade concrete. I may have you jackhammer it out and replace it. This on top of the long list of problems we gave you last week."

"You're just a hard ass, McGowin. I've been in this business for twenty years, and nobody's ever questioned my work like you do. I have to take all of this up with Sweeney. He's always been happy with my work."

"You do that! And remember, the anchor tenant is complaining about the cheap cabinetwork in the executive suites. He's watching everything you do because he's thinking of buying the building. He may demand replacement of those cabinets as well. And, Halloran, no more cost overruns without signed changes to the work order. As far as your twenty years of experience, I think it must have been one year experienced twenty times. Swenco has been notified that progress payments will be delayed until I sign off on all work from this point forward."

Damn, now he knows why this guy never ran one of McGowin's jobs before. Swenco must be having trouble. The bid was not awarded to them because of low price. Quality from this contractor, which had the winning bid but not the low bid, was paramount. As McGowin Corporation's executive vice president for engineering, design, and construction, Mike had never allowed shortcuts or lower-grade materials.

<hr />

He took time to cool down. He stretched his back muscle some more and shifted his efforts to a second major project taking up much of his time. He leaned over a large print table for an hour, compared progress at the construction site to drawings for the remodel of the ninety-thousand-square-foot Wilshire Property. The older building has needed attention for a long time. The improvement brought it up to date and helped retain some of the legacy firms up for renewal. Mike walked down the hall to the office of his sister Sally. At age thirty-eight, she's the chief financial officer of McGowin Corporation. He walked through the accounting office where several people were busy at computers, working their magic. He nodded and smiled warmly at Ann, Sally's secretary, walked to Sally's long leather couch, stretched himself out, and took up the full length of the furniture. Mike's Army reserve unit was activated in 2012 and sent to Afghanistan for a year. He suffered a moderate injury while aiding a more seriously injured comrade. A single sliver of metal from an exploding RPG penetrated his back near the spinal cord, causing temporary paralysis and muscle damage.

Sally hung up the phone. "How's the back?"

"It's okay, Sal. The muscles are still a little soft, but everything's coming back. I did a little too much bending over the drafting table today. The regular workout has made a huge difference. Sal, I'm sending Joel up to the *Blue Dolphin* next week to get her ready for the trip to the Sea of Cortez. She may be out of the country for as long as a month. This trip we have planned requires some prep work."

Sally said, "I'm glad Joel will be onboard to relieve you. He's an experienced seaman, a trained navigator, and damn good with those updated electronics you added."

"I suppose all of you plan on flying to Cabo and back?"

"That's the plan, Mike. However, Brett pressed us to let him go with you and Joel on the trip south to Cabo. He'll fly back to Los Angeles with the rest of us. Is that all right with you?"

"Of course, I'd love having Brett along. It's a long trip down the coast of Mexico. He can pull duty as Joel's assistant. How about Gayle, Robert, and the girls? Are all making the trip?"

"Robert is in litigation and can't get away, but Gayle and the girls can't wait to leave LA. Of course, Brett and Samantha are going."

Gayle, forty-two years old, is president and chief administrative officer of the family-owned corporation. Her children are Tanya and Sara.

"That's all, Mike, unless you think we should have Barbara along to take charge of the galley. After last year's trip to Catalina, I think she's hoping to be asked again this year. Dad's guilty of dropping hints to both she and Gayle about having her onboard. She's like another daughter to him. We're crazy about her too, and she especially likes you."

Mike said, "How about organizing a family dinner for one night?"

"As soon as Gayle returns from San Francisco, we'll get together," Sally said. "Is Joel sleeping in the upper salon again?"

"Yes, you know how he is. He calls that his sea cabin, and hardly sleeps at sea or on anchor. He keeps his gear in the large locker forward of the bridge."

Blue Dolphin, an eighty-five-foot classically designed custom-built cruising yacht, was designed by and built for Mike's father, Marcus McGowin. It was launched in 1990, built for long-range cruising, then recently refurbished and repowered with twin twelve-cylinder 850 HP diesel engines and pod drive systems. The turbo charged after cooled engines and new pod drive systems capable of pushing the reinforced aluminum hull craft beyond twenty knots.

Sally said, "Dad is eighty-five years old and would enjoy this trip again, don't you think?"

Mike hesitated. "He's resigned himself to the age factor now, Sal, satisfied with the monthly cruise to Avalon Harbor. He and longtime buddies meet to tell sea stories, drink good wine, and enjoy an occasional cigar. I think he just loves to talk about the Sea of Cortez with his fishing buddies. That's about it."

Sally said, "You likely won't be available for the regular board meeting on June 21. I called a special meeting of the board to obtain required approval before moving ahead with the three new projects scheduled to start early next year."

"Your design summaries and cost estimates require board approval, Mike. I was able to confirm a time for the special board meeting tomorrow morning at ten. I hope that gives you time to prepare. It will be a short meeting."

"That's fine. We do what we must."

Mike had another early-morning walkthrough at the construction site. He arrived late for the board meeting. Never shy about walking through the corporate office in work clothes (often blue jeans, T-shirt and heavy work shoes), he rushed through, down a hallway, past his own office, and into the executive locker rooms for a quick shower and change of clothes. The chairman's a stickler for the corporate dress code at all board functions.

He tucked in a freshly laundered shirt, tightened his tie, and pulled on a tailored light-gray Italian suit jacket. He passed Ann again on his way to the boardroom.

She said, "Good morning, Mike," without looking. "Your sisters are waiting for you in the boardroom." He was greeted by other staff members as he hurried through the office.

Oh well, looks like Ann's pissed at me. Haven't called her lately.

"Well, look what the cat dragged in!" said Sally as Mike entered the boardroom. "I wonder if the board would take you seriously if they saw you thirty minutes ago in your usual attire." Several board members greeted the late arrival in a friendly manner.

"Fortunately, he cleans up well," said Gayle.

"Thank you, ladies. All in the line of duty." Gayle and Sally finished up with a variety of issues of interest to the board.

Sally asked, "Did you talk to Joel? He's having more quality control issues with Swenco, and they had quite a row earlier today."

"I talked with him on the way here. That's one general contractor who's going to find his ass on the street if he gives any more trouble. If we have to, we can line up our own subs and finish the job ourselves. Joel's documented enough problems and shortcuts to stop any lawsuit, if it goes in that direction."

The board meeting was called to order. Chairman of the Board Marcus McGowin addressed Mike. "Those issues requiring board approval should be brought forward now, Mike. Myself and some of the other members have another pressing meeting to attend before noon. We'll address these issues and take our leave."

Mike presented the design revisions and new cost esti-mates for a previously approved forty-five-unit apartment complex to be built next year in Santa Monica. Also requiring board approval was the purchase of a five-acre tract of raw land in North Malibu. After a brief discussion, approval was granted. Other less critical new projects were pushed back until next year.

It was a productive meeting with no further business before the board. A motion to adjourn was made, seconded, and carried. Then board members departed.

Lingering in the boardroom, Gayle said to Mike, "You have a lot on your plate. How do we handle things while you're in Mexico?"

"Well, Gayle, our old-time construction foremen and the property managers have plans to keep you all up to date here in the corporate offices. That's how we've always handled it. Of course, I'll have telephone capabilities, and both Joel and I'll stay in touch with project foremen as usual. I certainly hope to have the Swenco problem solved one way or another before leaving town. I have a meeting with the president and his major shareholders Tuesday. I expect to have the construction superintendent replaced with a man we've worked with in the past. He's now on another Swenco project, but that's their only option. As you know, all our people have been with us for many years and are loyal to the company. I trust their judgment, and they're not afraid of responsibility."

Sally interrupted, "Now! Let's get to the important stuff and talk about our trip to Mexico."

CHAPTER 5

Lance Howell, Cabo

June 10, 2015

Ladies' man, Lance Howell struggled to rise from the piss-covered floor, his blue eyes and blond hair filled with his own blood. He yelled to his henchmen, "Get those goddamn women in the van and tie them up good. Now, before that bastard tries to interfere again! And get me some help here. I'm hurt. I'm gone kill that big sonabitch."

The women tried to hide in the ladies' room, pleading with a Caucasian patron. "Help us! Men out there tried to force us to go with them!" screamed the tall woman with one eye swollen shut. "Is there an exit out the rear?" said the other. "These men want to kidnap us, maybe kill us. Please, we're all alone here."

Startled, the young woman turned toward the rear cubicle to answer, was grabbed, and violently shaken by one of the pursuers.

Lance's hired strongmen, brothers Hondo and Duck, had rushed into the ladies' room without consideration for any women who were compromised.

Duck slammed into the stalls one after the other. Hondo held the young white female at the mirror. Duck yelled out, "Got-um!" Both men crowded into the restroom stall, attempting to subdue the two women. The tall dark-haired woman kicked and fought violently, landing a hard kick to Duck's crotch. He backed out of the cubicle, cursing loudly.

Hondo saw the damage to his brother, slammed an elbow hard to the woman's face, and knocked her back against the other. Within minutes, both women were dragged outside through a side door, shoved into an old Ford van, and tied to seats behind the driver. Still fighting, they were taken to a dirty little warehouse near the marina and locked in a small dark room with one bare mattress on a rusty bed frame. A tiny cubicle in the corner provided a commode and sink.

Duck said, "I'd like to kick the shit out o' that big woman. I don't care how much she's worth. My nuts hurt."

"Lance would kill you. This is business to him, and his orders were clear. Don't damage the goods! You know we get a crack at them only if his deal falls through."

"I don't know about you, big brother, but I've had enough of Lance's dirty work. One more year of his shit and I can kick back with all the women I want."

"You ain't going nowhere, and you know it. The money's too good. Now, take a look around outside. We can't go aboard the boat until the whole damn marina is asleep."

Frightened and battered, Tracy and Stephanie sat on a dirty mattress, holding each other.

Stephanie said, "I'm sorry I got you involved in this mess. You've always been there to bail me out of trouble. Now if something happens to both of us, it'll kill Mom and Dad."

"We can't think like that, damn it. This toilet tissue is soaked with blood. Will you see if there's any by the toilet? My nose won't stop bleeding."

Stephanie answered, "Shit, shit, shit. There's no paper, and there's not even a seat on this filthy toilet. I have to pee so bad, my knees are shaking."

"Just spread your legs and go anyway. Don't waste a thought about going on the floor. At least we can't see the bugs in here without lights."

Hours later, Hondo opened the door and flashed a bright light directly into the faces of the frightened women. "You come easy. I'll only tie your hands in front. You act up, I'll stuff your underwear in your mouth and put a hood over your head. What's it going to be?"

"We'll go along quietly if you'll treat us properly. We're tired, hungry, and I need first-aid treatment."

Howell's fleet of feeder vessels rendezvoused with a huge freighter that transported cartel drugs and human cargo. Small panga boats were preloaded and dropped at various points along the California coast.

Lance phoned his assistant, Augustine Palmyra, at the main office and distribution center in Port San Quentin. "I'm hospitalized with serious injuries in Cabo. The payment for that last shipment is past due. Listen up, August. I want you to get hold of the Guerrero brothers as soon as possible. They should be back aboard my yacht in Cabo by now, with some very valuable cargo that's to be offered up through the usual channels. Have them call my cell number in exactly two hours. I'm doing everything possible to get out of this fucking hospital. I can talk business with them when I have the privacy of my own vehicle. Make damn sure they keep trying to reach me."

Later, he answered the phone. From his SUV, he bellowed into his cell, "God damn it, Hondo, you heard what I said. You and Duck are going to have to take full responsibility for this trip. You've made it with me often enough to handle it right, and that means absolutely no screw-ups. You have the payoff money onboard and your expense money. I expect my yacht to be returned in the same shape it's in now—excellent. Don't let that half-million-dollar payment for the shippers tempt you."

Hondo said, "Boss, I don't want to do this. That's a big ocean. I might not be able to find the island."

"I showed you how to use the GPS. You've taken the boat out four or five times with me along, didn't need my help. You're being paid well, so don't give me any crap. My penalty for betrayal is painful before you die. Listen carefully now. I'm going to say it one more time. The women are to be fed and cared for without more brutality. They may prove very valuable. Until I'm sure of the deal, you're responsible for their well-being. It's possible that you'll have to dispose of them at sea if the sale doesn't work out. You have all of the waypoint information for the rendezvous? Yes, there in the pilot house. Yes. Again, if disposal is necessary, you may have them as you like. Then wrap the bodies in chain and dump them in deep water far from land. Do not move in that direction until I tell you to."

Lance's yacht, *Sly Fox*, traveled all day on a course of 330 degrees, with moderate winds and a five-foot swell out of the west. The powerful sport fisher sliced through the seas with ease. Not so for the women locked in a small stateroom.

Hondo instructed Duck, "Go see to the women. If they agree to my terms and cause no problems, let them into the galley and salon. You keep your pants zipped up. We have plenty of time for that."

Duck unlocked the door of the starboard guest suite where the sisters were fighting nausea and fear of the unknown. He looked down at the tall woman. "We may allow you into the galley and salon. First, you agree to make coffee, sandwiches, and help out when we ask. Most important, you cause no problems and follow orders at once. You agree?"

"Do we have any other choice?"

"Not unless you want to be locked in this room for many days."

"We'll be meeting with other men in thirty-six hours. You'll have freedom until then. But you must stay quiet in your room when the men come aboard. You understand?"

"We'll do what you say and cause no trouble as long as you don't try to hurt us."

CHAPTER 6

Sea of Cortez, La Paz, Mexico

May 30, 2015

Blue Dolphin lay secure in her berth at Marina Cortez, having logged fourteen hundred nautical miles in seventy-eight hours.

Fifteen-year-old Brett Robinson reached for his water bottle, downed half the bottle, and yelled out, "Hey, Mike! I thought we were going ashore for lunch."

"After four eggs, hash browns, and six pancakes, surely you can hold out till noon. It's only 11:10."

Brett, tall for his age, already looked down on his five-ten mother. His father, Phil, was six-one, with wide shoulders and long legs. A very good college athlete in his own right. *This kid's going to be a hell of a linebacker*, thought Mike.

"Get on the intercom, Brett, and locate Joel. He's in the engine room. See if he can join us for lunch before the family gets in."

Lunch about over, Brett finished a tall ice tea, asked for a refill, dug into his second cheeseburger and fries. Mike and Joel had a Mexican beer, relaxed under the outside umbrella, and waited. "So you couldn't find the spark plugs on the diesel engines," Mike said.

Brett nodded his understanding. "Until Joel said diesels don't have plugs and explained why. How was my navigation on the trip down?"

"You did well reading the chart and calculating the course using the parallel rule and compass rose. We'll sign you up for celestial navigation next year."

Joel said, "What time are we picking up the fly-ins?"

"Their plane arrives at 1:14. We have just enough time for lunch then make the airport. Do you want to pick them up?" Mike said.

Mike and Brett sat under the umbrella at Café Capri, glancing occasionally toward the hot parking lot. Mike looked at his heavy black dive watch, signaled for fresh drinks, and saw a white Dodge van pull into the parking lot. Doors on both sides flew open immediately, and three tall, attractive teenage girls ran toward Mike and Brett, leaving Joel to remove the luggage and close up the van. A lot of hugging and kissing. Mike sent Brett over to help Joel with the luggage.

Mike looked at Samantha. "Did you lose somebody on the way over?"

"Oh! You know my mom. She wanted to visit her favorite cantina on the way from the airport. Uncle Phil insisted that all of the adults follow in a taxi."

Mike said, "All you guys, listen up for a minute. Remember now, the first hour of the cruise tomorrow we'll hold our usual emergency drill, including the man-overboard exercise. That's when we throw Brett overboard for the drill."

Brett said, "Great, I get to dunk all the girls while they're in the water."

Mike eased the tender up to the dinghy dock where the wayward crew members stood in the hot sun. Phil grabbed the rail and held the tender tight against the dock so the others could board safely.

Barbara placed her hands on Mike's shoulders and kissed him on the forehead. "Hi, Muscles. Your father said stop by for a brandy when you return. He loves hearing about the grandkids."

Mike grabbed a small bag and eased the attractive forty-three-year-old widow and longtime family friend to a seat forward in the tender. Barbara Blair and her husband owned a successful waterfront restaurant in Ventura Harbor. After her husband lost his life night diving for lobster near Santa Cruz Island, she sold the restaurant and went to work for Marcus McGowin. As a trusted friend, she managed the estate for the elderly family patriarch, residing in her own private quarters at the family home in Mandalay Bay.

Mike said, "Okay now, how many margaritas did you have?"

Barbara laughed. "I can still navigate these waters, mate, so trim your jib and let's get underway."

Sally and Gayle laughed out loud, trying not to drop the two margaritas they were holding, splashing Phil, trying to keep them from falling in the water.

Barbara looked at Mike. "Don't you even think about casting off tomorrow, Captain Bligh, until I check the stores aboard and put my brand of approval on the galley!"

Mike and Phil stopped in the main salon and saw Gayle and Sally poking around the wet bar. They had changed into tropical attire, bikini swimsuits.

Mike said, "I thought for a minute there I was looking at Samantha and Sara checking out the bar stock."

Gayle said, "I better not see those two nosing around here for a few more years."

"Why not? Remember when Dad found out you and Sally were watering down the vodka bottle?"

"All right, but we weren't the only ones. You just didn't get caught."

An hour out of La Paz, Mike pointed to a tiny yellow canary that flew in through the open door of the upper salon and perched himself on a rack full of martini glasses over the bar.

Gayle said, "He's waiting for happy hour."

The fascinating little guy sat above the bar ten minutes, unafraid of his human companions, then circled around the room a couple of times before settling on the top of an open door. Later, he flew away as casually as he arrived.

Mike thought, *I've seen these little guys' miles at sea many times. Where do they come from?*

He eased *Blue Dolphin* into the calm anchorage on the lee side of the small island an hour before sunset. The crew rushed to the railing and looked down at the magnificent clear water filled with a variety of active sea life, every bit as curious about the visitors as the other way around.

Phil said, "Open up all the doors, latch them back, and open up down below. The dry, light breeze is perfect inside or out. We can do without the air conditioning."

The entire vessel was a beehive of activity. Mike set the ship's GPS anchor alarm, checked all power systems, and declared he and Joel to be off duty.

The ship's power generators, designed with a dry stack exhaust system, vented the pre-cooled, muffled exhaust quietly out through the hollow superstructure. The design prevented exposing swimmers in the water to the generators' deadly exhaust gases.

Brett led the team of snorkelers to the dive compartment and passed out snorkel gear to the young people. They rushed to enter the warm water. Several large dive bags were left scattered around the cockpit.

Sally pointed. "Look at that. A curious trio of dolphin moved in to investigate the strange activity."

Tanya, in the water, screamed with delight. "That one came close enough for me to slide my fingers along her slippery side. Mom, you should see all the fish down there."

The adults toasted the great weather with their first cocktail of the day.

Smiling, Sally said to Joel, "Activate the com system, please, so we can spy on the activity in the water."

The sensitive microphones for this system were placed strategically throughout the vessel, relayed voices to the bridge speakers, or passed them to specific points inside or outside the vessel.

Joel flipped a few switches in the console above the helm, and the madcap activity emerged from a recessed speaker beneath the lip of the superstructure. He triggered another switch, and bright underwater lights illuminated the darkening water beneath and around *Blue Dolphin.*

The kids in the water appeared shocked to see the sudden bright light reflected off a white sandy bottom and the variety of sea life crowding around them.

Mike thought, *This is why dad loved the Baja area so much.*

Mike rose early, coaxed a first cup of bold coffee from the single cup machine, and walked outside. He was shocked to see four adults already enjoying the sundeck. A thin veil of morning haze blocked some of the brilliance from the morning sun emerging out of the Sea of Cortez. "What's going on? You guys are too quiet."

Barbara said, "Life can't get any better. So don't tell me we're leaving again."

"No, Barbara! Enjoy it while you can. The kids are going to be out early."

He noticed a sea tray loaded with Bloody Mary fixings, untouched, but tempting.

Barbara said, "Omelets for the adults, walnut pancakes for the kids in one hour."

***

Mike chose another good dive site for the next early-morning anchor drop. He and Joel assisted the young scuba divers get suited up.

Mike said, "Listen up, everyone, just for a minute. This is your first dive this trip. I know we've all been on many dives together, but just remember the basics. We're anchored in only forty feet of clear warm water. The visibility should be excellent wherever you go. Remember, even on a shallow dive, follow behind your bubbles when returning to the surface."

He pointed at Sara. "You sometimes forget to keep your eye on your air pressure gauge and come up struggling for air. Don't forget again. Always know your depth and the amount of air in your tank. Brett has more experience, so he should lead on this dive, with Samantha in the rear. Tanya, you and Sara spread out behind Brett."

He looked to see if they were paying attention. "Samantha will follow behind and between, taking pictures, tail o' the fish. Try to keep each other in sight. Now, if you see something to be checked out on the bottom it slows the dive, tap on your tank a few times, not the rapid danger signal, but slowly. Always respond to a tapping signal. Now, listen up, the big old sailboat beneath where you were snorkeling earlier is about thirty feet deep, so you can look it over. However, never attempt to enter or reach inside any opening where an unexpected inhabitant might be located."

Mike swallowed some beer. "I'll be in the tender above following your bubbles. If there's any problem at all, surface slowly, and I'll be there. You each have 2,300 pounds of air. That should give you enough for a nice swim over the bottom. I would like to see 500 pounds remaining so I know you are watching your gauges. Any questions?"

Mike guided the tender over the divers. They followed a small school of large colorful fish, always just out of their reach. He watched the scene below in the crystal-clear water until his view became obstructed by their air bubbles. After an hour, Mike, feeling the hot sun, needed a cold beer. He saw the dive leader pop to the surface.

Sara and Tanya chatted away about this one or that one followed through the shallow canyons. Sara climbed over the short dive ladder and dropped her tank, laughing. "Some of those darn fish kept nibbling at my freckles."

Tanya said, "That big yellow one really liked you, Sara. I almost touched him a couple of times."

The next day, Mike made a scenic cruise around Isla San Jose and approached the chosen anchorage at midday. *Another small island ideal for the water toys,* he thought. *We can spend a couple nights here before our stop at Espiritu Santo.*

He called Sally and Gayle in from the foredeck. "It's so hot in the middle of the day. Let's rest up, kick back another couple of hours, and let the sun drop a bit before turning the kids loose."

Mike relaxed with a beer and watched the kids race wet bikes. He looked back to the rear and saw Phil, Sally, and Gayle with water skis board the tender from the swim platform, ready to rumble.

He thought, *A full day and two nights just evaporated like dew in the morning sun.*

━━∽∼∿∼∽━━

Mike announced loudly over the intercom, "All of you asleep in the sun, look out at the beauty before you. That's Isla Espiritu Santo you've all been waiting for."

Everybody jumped up and moved to the starboard railing to get a look at the clear water cove and white sandy beach.

Gayle slapped Mike on the arm. "You did it again, fella, another great choice anchorage. Just look at those tiny waves hitting the beach. How deep is it, Mike?"

"Only thirty-five feet, Gayle, a young diver's paradise." Mike recalled diving here with his father at age fifteen. He put on an old beat-up wide brim straw hat and watched the divers suit up. He saw they were ready and climbed aboard the tender.

"Listen up, guys and gals, you may find this interesting. My dad dived with me here when I was fifteen years old. I've measured all other dive sites against this one for years. None ever replaced it as my favorite. Hope you will like it too. Expect a lot of narrow shallow canyons leading out away from the cove, all full of fish."

He followed over the divers with the tender. The bottom was mostly rocky, with enough white sand to reflect light, making visibility excellent. Long shimmering sea grasses helped camouflage the many varieties of colorful fish. Large manta rays swam over the bottom, seemingly unafraid of the divers and their constant cavalcade of air bubbles tumbling toward the surface. The forever-present sea lions were no longer afraid and came in close, evermore curious. A large bait ball spun toward the divers, threatened to engulf them,

44

only to spin away, shimmering in the sunlight from above. Some of the schooling fish were as long as a man's arm. Many fish with bright yellow tails swam close and nibbled at exposed flesh—not breaking the skin, but still scary. Once, a pair of dolphin swam close to examine the divers, looking straight into the face plate of some divers before swimming away.

Sara removed her dive mask and yelled at Mike, "This was the best dive ever, Mike. I can't wait to see the pictures on the big screen. Sam got an awesome picture of Brett riding a giant bat ray."

She tossed her face plate and fins into the tender. "That one shot of Tanya coming out of the bait ball has got to be a good one too."

"What would you say about putting into port overnight at La Paz?" Sally said.

"Hey, that's up to you and Gayle. I'm always flexible with these things." Mike knew the fine Mexican restaurants were too tempting for his sisters.

Blue Dolphin, berthed on an outer section of the harbor, provided a beautiful unobstructed view into the bay of La Paz.

Mike said, "Barbara, I know how you feel about missing out on another big meal aboard, but I've made seven-o'clock reservations for everyone at Las Tres Vergennes restaurant across town. I can make it up to you by letting you prepare me a large chicken fried steak and egg breakfast tomorrow, if it'll make you feel better."

Barbara reached across, grabbed Mike's cap, and slapped it down hard across the top of his head a couple of times. "You just can't stay out of trouble, can you?" Moments later, Barbara returned with the coffee decanter, refilled all three cups, left, returned again with two large pieces of peach pie smothered with ice cream. She placed a much-smaller piece on the table for herself. "There's no use leaving tonight's dessert, is there?"

Joel said, "Barbara, you have to marry me. I'm spoiled already for anyone else. Mike, as captain of the ship, can you perform the ceremony?"

"Yes, I can! However, the ceremony is only good for the duration of the cruise."

"Perfect! Then how about it, Barbara?"

"No chance, Prince Charming. It's got to be a life sentence or none at all."

"Why haven't you married again anyway, Barbara? You're still young and attractive."

"I don't know. Maybe I feel like Marcus McGowin. He said life only gets better when the last child leaves home and old Rover dies. I was never fortunate enough to have children, but life's good, so maybe I've reached that point."

Mike said, "Not so, Barbara. You just might turn around one day and feel that thrill of romance again. Look at the three of us sitting here, all single. Are any of you really ready to give up the quest? I don't think so."

"Our last night here," Mike said. "Samantha! Get your camera. We will all line up on deck for the family picture. Dad's album has pictures of every trip to Mexico."

CHAPTER 7

Cabo San Lucas

June 10, 2015

Onboard *Blue Dolphin*, Mike McGowin spread several navigation charts across the table. "Joel, the course is set from twenty miles out for good coastal clearance. The coastline of the Baha Peninsula runs approximately 335 degrees north by northwest. We'll have a straight six-hundred-mile run, slipping between Alijos Rocks and Rosa Banks. Then a straight shot outside Isla Cerros on a heading of 155 degrees. We can plug into the system and get ETA, fuel usage, and a more accurate plot before shoving off."

Joel said, "I finished the engine room check this morning. Both generators have performed well, although the small 12 KW needs servicing. It's been running twenty-four hours a day for that damn water maker."

"With only two of us aboard, we shouldn't need to make more water for a week or so. How about the Cats? Have you noticed more high temperatures on the portside?"

"No problem since I cleaned seaweed out of the saltwater intake filter. Those damn twelve-cylinder beasts don't miss a beat. We averaged twenty knots at 2,800 RPM down the sea of Cortez. Even at 3,200, the turbo temp only climbed one degree. Also, we took on an additional 2,300 gallons of number 2 diesel fuel. That should leave some cheap fuel for use in the home waters."

"How about finishing up your chores, so we can go ashore for one last good Mexican dinner before leaving Mexico?"

"You're a gringo after my own heart, Mike. I know just the place. It's four or five miles from the marina, so we'll have to grab a cab. It has damn good Mexican food, and the Mexican beer ain't bad either. It's always popular with expatriate Americans, though, and occasionally has a little dustup. If anybody picks on you, Mike, I'll whip his ass. After all, I did promise your old man I'd look after you down here."

Dressed in fishing shorts and T-shirt, Mikes' six-foot four-inch, 235-pound frame and muscular thighs left the outer seams ripped at the bottom. His muscular torso stressed the well-worn T-shirt.

"Why, you little shit, Joel, you couldn't weigh more than a buck sixty. But you do remind me of a firmly packed watch-it."

"What the hell is a watch-it?"

"A watch-it, my cocky friend, is ten pounds of shit in a five-pound bag. If one comes your way, you better know what to do." He was a tough little shit, few small scars around his eyes from his golden glove days.

"Aw, come on now, what you really mean is two hundred pounds of tiger packed into a hundred-sixty-pound body."

<hr>

After a fifteen-minute taxi ride, the two friends entered a decent-looking moderately busy restaurant.

Joel pointed to a table near the dance floor where people were leaving. "There's an open table."

"Let's get farther away from the loud music, maybe that booth in the center rear. It's open." The booth was small, intended for four people. Mike shoved the table closer to

Joel's side and sat down. Most people at the bar were smoking, but so far, the smoke was not bad.

"It's clear to see why you like this place, Joel. All the bar maids wear string bikinis. And look there, the food servers have on short white aprons in front. I do wonder, what could they be hiding under there?"

The fish-house-style decor is surprisingly well done with various nets, flotation devices, lobster traps, and a variety of mounted sea life.

Joel said, "Order us up a couple of cadillac margaritas while I hit the head."

Mike looked around. This place was no different from a hundred watering holes he had parked his butt in around the world. Change the language and the music a little, and he was back in any one of them.

He saw several "blue moons" at the bar. Beyond those girls were some tough-looking men drinking heavy. That table in the dimly lit corner had all the ingredients for trouble—two attractive gringo women, one gringo male, and a couple of tough-looking Mexican men.

The two women stood and attempted to leave. The big gringo yelled out, "Sit down, damn it!" and downed a shot of tequila. One man smirked, stood, and pushed the blonde woman back down into her chair. The tall brunette slapped the white guy hard across the face, a sound like a rifle shot. The white guy reached across the table and delivered a blow to the woman's temple, sending her to the floor out of sight.

Damn! I sure called that one, he thought. Standing, Mike said, "This is not our problem, Joel, but I hate shitheads who abuse women. It's time for a little retribution. Pay the check so we can get out of here on our own terms."

Throwing money on the table, Joel said, "You'd better get your attention on something besides that blonde over there. The cocktail girl said that big white guy and the Mexicans are known narco."

Mike wanted a better look at that dark-haired girl. It's so damn dark in that corner. Had only an occasional side view of a classic profile and full lips. That always got to him. He didn't understand women who put themselves in situations like that.

"You're going to get our asses in trouble—deep trouble. This isn't our territory. We're all alone down here, and I don't like Mexican jails." Joel grabbed Mike's arm. "Wait. He's headed away from the others. Okay, take care of business, if you have to, while I offer my help, even if it gets my ass kicked."

Mike waited a few moments, walked toward the men's room down a narrow dim hallway, listened at the door, heard water running, no conversation, and entered.

The woman beater turned to face him and grinned, expecting trouble.

He ignored the grin, moved fast as the thug opened a long switch blade and lunged. Mike stepped to the left and slammed his right foot hard into the man's exposed rib cage. Cracked ribs sounded like a face slap. Mike knew several were busted. The blow sent the man hard against the porcelain urinal where he collapsed to the dirty floor, gasping for breath. Mike reached down, picked up the knife, wedged the blade into a crack in the block wall, pressed down on the handle, and snapped the blade off.

Grimacing in pain, the hoodlum growled at Mike, "You don't know who I am, asshole. You won't get out of here in one piece."

Mike looked into the man's eyes, grabbed his head with both hands, and slammed his face hard against the piss-covered floor. Piss and blood splattered on the wall around the urinal. "The ribs are for the women you've just abused. The face is for the threat you made to me."

He left the men's room. He didn't see the women but saw the two Mexican men facing off with Joel, and he headed toward them.

The big man with a mean look sent the two thugs away, past the bar and down another dim hallway toward the ladies' room. "Let's get the hell out of here, Joel. Trouble is on its way. That guy is in no condition to be chasing those women around now. They should be fine, but we may have a posse after us soon. Leaving Cabo San Lucas at zero dark thirty could be a good idea, Joel."

"Oh yeah. It didn't take us long to get into trouble, did it?"

Mike and Joel walked to a small convenience store, spotted a cab, were dropped off within a mile of the Baha marina, and walked to the boat from there. What the hell have I got us into now!

―――

Mike said, "You know, Joel, we'll be terribly busy once we get back to Los Angeles. I have a corporate board meeting on the twenty-first that requires some prep work. Then we start the remodel on the Wilshire property. That means I'll be tied up through the rest of the year, and you, my friend, have five office buildings that you're responsible for. Regardless of that, something tells me that we should take our time about returning home and try to get a few more good dives in, weather permitting of course. This way, we'll be hiding in plain sight for a while."

"Okay, Mike, but I think it'd be a mistake to take those narco guys too lightly. That guy back there'll be turning over every rock in sight trying to find us. If he connects us with the *Blue Dolphin*, our asses are worm food."

"You're absolutely right. You know, I've always wanted to dive Guadalupe Island, but it seemed so far away. Maybe a side trip now would be appropriate and just might take us away from the action for a week or so."

He hesitated long enough to collect his thoughts. "The galley is loaded up, and fuel's not a problem. Guadalupe is certainly off the beaten path. Few vessels have the range for a round trip out that far."

"That it is," Joel added. "This might be the best time for a visit. I can have all of the dive tanks filled by the time we get there. We don't have a diver's guide for the island, do we?"

"We don't really need one, unless there's something spectacular we don't know about."

CHAPTER 8

Rescue at Sea

June 16, 2015

Mike picked up the nude woman and hugged her shivering body close to his own. Bare above his fishing shorts, he shared his body heat. He looked at the woman's bruised face, one eye swollen shut, the other peeking through her long dark hair. "Joel! Rush down below and bring up a couple of the thermal throws from the salon and nuke the rest of our morning coffee." *Can this be the same slim woman from the Cabo debacle? Didn't get a look at that girl's face. Yes! The same dark hair . . . full lips.* He picked up the slim figure and climbed the three short steps from the cockpit to the lazarette deck, where Joel met him with the warm wrap.

Joel wrapped the girl and tucked the blanket in between her naked body and Mike. He touched Mike's elbow, guided him into the salon, toward a soft L-shaped couch. Mike sat down in the corner and continued to hold the shivering woman.

"Bring the hot coffee, Joel. Add sugar and cream. It'll go down easier."

The woman tried to speak. She attempted to raise her head and be heard. One eye closed shut. The other strained to see through wet hair. She stared at Mike's whiskered face and struggled to speak again.

Mike felt her rapid heartbeat and short breaths and spoke to her, this time quite loud, "Look, hon, you have to take long, slow breaths. Concentrate on that. Then we'll give you a little warm coffee."

She attempted to speak again, but failed. Her eyes would not leave Mike's face.

He looked down at the troubled face again, startled with recognition. "Oh, goddamn, no, no, no! Tracy, is it you? Tracy, please! Nod your head!" He brushed her hair away.

She moved her head up and down. Tears eased from the inside corner of her gorgeous green eyes. Mike pulled her close, rocking back and forth. His own tears wetted his sun-darkened cheeks. He raised his head and in a low voice said, "Thank you, God. I will never doubt you again."

Joel, holding a decanter of coffee and several coffee mugs on a wooden tray, stood staring down on the confusing scene. He placed the tray on the nearby coffee table. "What in the hell is happening, Mike? I've never seen anything like it. Tell me, so I can help."

Mike looked up at Joel. "You won't believe it, Joel. I'll fill you in after we get moving. We should get underway first at a reasonable pace. Set the autopilot and come back so I can fill you in. I'm sure now. She's going to make it."

Tracy's breathing smoothed out. She reached up, attempted to put her arm around Mike's thick neck, snuggled into his chest, and shed more tears as convulsive reflexes racked her slim body. She struggled again to get a few words out, to be understood. "My sister . . . Don't call authorities . . . Kill her."

Mike soon understood the few words from Tracy. "Don't call authorities. It'd mean death for my sister." He made an effort to pour coffee. Tracy held him tight, not ready to move out of the security of Mike's strong embrace.

Joel poured two steaming cups of coffee, hoping to draw information from Mike. "We're still on our set course of

155 degrees, making only about eight knots. I think we need to know what's going on before we rush out ahead."

Mike reached out with one hand for the coffee. "You won't believe the miracle. This battered little refugee you're looking at has been one of the most important people in my life." He tried to coax some warm coffee between Tracy's lips. "We met and fell in love many years ago, then let life interfere. I prayed to have God bring her back into my life, so many lonely nights. I'm convinced this horrific situation is no less than a miracle. Can't lose her now. I'm afraid we have some serious problems to face before this blessing's understood."

Joel poured a second cup for Mike. "We didn't know, Mike."

"Unfortunately for Tracy, Joel, we were unaware of just what was going on back in Cabo San Lucas when we tucked tail and sailed. We've been given a second chance to save her life. Her sister's fate is still an unknown. I don't know what to make of all this, but we have to count on Tracy to fill in the blanks."

Joel moved around and checked radar for other vessels.

Mike sipped his coffee and touched Tracy's damp scalp, feeling for damage. Tracy moved around better and became more coherent and responsive to his prompting. He lifted her bruised face, kissed the sunburned nose tenderly, and spoke in a soft voice, "Please, honey, we have to get as many facts as you can give us before we make an attempt to locate your sister. If you can sit up and talk to me, I can make you more comfortable and let you get some rest. Are you warming up?"

Tracy nodded, tried to sit up, struggled, made an effort to pull the warm blanket around full breasts, and pressed against Mike's bare chest. She looked at him from her battered face and tried to smile.

Mike pulled the blanket in between them, eased Tracy over to the side, and positioned her in the warm corner of the couch where he'd been sitting.

Joel passed a second cup of coffee for Tracy and returned to the helm station.

Mike eased the cup to her lips with his hand on the back of her matted hair. He helped Tracy's unsteady attempt to sip the warm liquid.

She looked at Mike. "Thank you. I have to get this all out in case something else happens. It was all about drugs. It must be a big operation." She looked around. "Mike, I need something to wear. Would you have something warm I could put on? I'm very uncomfortable without any clothing. I'm also embarrassed. You and your friend have done all you can to help me without making me feel worse."

Mike headed downstairs, turned, and smiled. "I've just what you need. He returned moments later with his arms full. I have two sisters who spend a great deal of time aboard, so you'll be able to find what you need once you're strong enough to move about. I couldn't resist the sweats though."

Tracy attempted to smile, reaching for a well-worn work-out suit. In spite of her effort to remain calm, tears trickled down her bruised cheekbone. "I'm very unsteady, Mike. Can you help me to someplace I can get dressed?"

Mike lifted her to her feet. She stood on weak legs, hugging the blanket. He helped her down two decks into the quiet master stateroom. "Look through those lockers and drawers. Feel free to use anything in here. After you're dressed, maybe you can answer a few questions."

"Yes. Please stay here with me. I just need a moment of privacy." She turned, tossed the blanket on the bed, and headed into the dressing room.

Mike watched Tracy walk away from him. He marveled at the long, perfect legs and body. He thought, *She has taken good care of herself, physically. I hope the rest of her life has been as well cared for. What else is new? Husband? Family? Children? All in due time, I suppose.*

After only five minutes or so, Tracy returned from dressing, looking much better. He led her up to the salon deck, then into the glass-enclosed pilot house.

Joel sat back in a captain's chair, nodded, and kept watching a few images of distant objects on a large radar screen.

Mike kept his eyes on Tracy. He was reminded again of that classic beauty and personal bearing that never seemed obvious to the girl.

The upper station was well equipped and comfortable for the crew. A soft leather couch sat on a raised platform behind the two identical high captain's chairs. Its length reached the port bulkhead where a teak table was secured beneath the large portside window and navigator's station. A full decanter of coffee and plate heaped with pastries looked inviting to mike.

He poured two cups of coffee, placed one on a tray near Tracy, wrapped a napkin around one of the cream-filled doughnuts, and set it within her easy reach.

Joel said, "Where's that waterlogged little thing that we plucked out of the Pacific Ocean?"

"Thanks with all my heart, Joel. I remember you offering help to my sister and me in Cabo. Thanks again for that."

Mike answered for Joel, "I hate to rush this, guys, but I have a strong feeling that time may be running out. We need to figure out what's going on as soon as possible."

~~~

Tracy began telling her story. "My younger sister, Stephanie, a middle school teacher in Santa Barbara, met this guy Lance Howell at a beach volleyball tournament and let herself get involved way too soon. I'll wait to fill in most details. She accepted an invitation for sun and sea that turned into a nightmare. She was scared, asked if I could fly to Cabo San Lucas at once. Her purse, with all personal possessions, had disappeared soon after meeting Lance at his boat. He kept promising to take care of everything. Frustration and suspicion led her to reach out for my help. I was the logical one to ask." Tracy accepted a sip of coffee and took a moment to catch her breath.

"I flew down at once and met Stephie and Lance at the small boat harbor where she directed me. Lance had a nice expensive-looking yacht. I felt everything was going to work out. Steph and I relaxed on the aft deck, enjoyed the beautiful weather, and tried to arrive at some logical answer to the problem."

Tracy drank a little more coffee. "Lance apologized for having to meet with business associates in the afternoon, soon left with the visitors. He returned later, asked us to dinner, said everything was all right. A man was meeting us at the restaurant with Stephanie's handbag. Later, when ready for dinner, I realized that my own purse with my return airline ticket and personal possessions was also missing. Lance said that he had friends joining us with everything. They were bringing one of the men who had visited Lance earlier. He had taken the bags but was returning them. We felt more or less at his mercy and agreed to stay only through dinner. Lance drove us to the restaurant in a nice SUV. Everything started to become more and more contentious as we questioned him and didn't like the answers we were getting. I suggested to Stephie that we leave and call a taxi. You know pretty much what happened afterwards at the restaurant."

Tracy asked for a glass of water. "As soon as Hondo and Duck Guerrero appeared at our table, I knew we were in trouble. We stood up to leave when Lance demanded that we sit down and stay put. I stood again and slapped him hard across the face. He became furious and hit me back, hard. We were told he'd make the decisions for both of us. We'd have no choice. Hondo and Duck dragged us out and tied us in one of the rear seats of some old van. We were taken to an old dirty warehouse until after dark, then to Lance's boat where we were locked in a small cabin with two beds and a toilet. That's where we stayed. Duck brought in rice and beans with two water bottles twice a day."

Tracy drank some water. "Sometime, the second day, we heard the motors start. Several people were talking loud. From there, I sort of lost track of what was going on. We went fast all day and night. The air in our cabin was stale, and the boat was pounding hard against the waves. We were both sick the whole time. We tried to sleep. Then one of the men came down and told us he would release us with the full freedom of the boat if we'd cooperate and cause no trouble. We were given crew duties and allowed to move about the boat. I heard them use the radio a lot, and they had some kind of special telephone. They talked to Lance. I could hear them talking to each other from the salon. They often talked to other ships or boats. It became obvious that drugs and people were being moved around on boats they called pangas. They were afraid of Lance but couldn't understand why they couldn't have fun with Steph and me."

She stopped for a moment. "On the second or third day at sea, they locked us in our cabin and told us to be quiet or they wouldn't be responsible for what might happen to us. We could hear a lot of loud talking in Spanish and talking on the phone. That went on all day. We heard other boat motors start up, and pretty soon, our boat started up. We were later released and told to prepare food and coffee. I felt like we cruised all night. About 4:00 AM, Duck came down to the galley for coffee. I heard Hondo above on the phone. It was clear he was talking to Lance. It became obvious things were changing."

Tracy wiped her tears away. "Duck went down below the aft deck and brought up a small anchor and some chain. I thought we might be going to anchor near an island I'd seen two or three times over the last few days. Then I heard Hondo tell Duck to go ahead with the dark-haired woman. I panicked and waked Stephie. Duck came into our cabin and tried to tie us both up again. We started screaming and fighting. Duck called to Hondo for help, and they tied our hands in front of us. Hondo locked Steph in the cabin, and Duck went back to the boat controls."

Tracy reached for another tissue. "Hondo dragged me into the salon and violently stripped all my clothing off, including my underwear. I heard Duck calling Hondo, telling him to come to the radio. That's when I broke away and ran out on the deck."

She looked at Mike. "I was sure they were going to rape me and tie the anchor around my body before shoving me overboard. I heard Stephie screaming and slamming herself against the door. I looked up and saw the silhouette of the island in the moonlight. It looked so near. I'm a very good swimmer and felt like taking this last gamble was much better than the alternative. The island seemed so close yet so far."

She raised her face away from Mike's shoulder. "I jumped, turned on my back, and kicked with my legs. Sometimes I would stop to rest with just my face out of the water. The sky started getting brighter, and I was so afraid they would turn around and come back for me. The last time I looked toward the boat, it was fading away into the dark. I soon realized that my body temperature was dropping. I could feel myself tiring. Then I spotted a thick patch of kelp.

I thought maybe it would keep me afloat while I rested, didn't hear your boat until just before I turned and saw a huge unshaven man looking at me."

Mike and Joel stared at Tracy, obviously fascinated.

Mike took Tracy in his arms and held her ever so close. So many questions to ask. "Tracy, we have to act on this problem right away. You've been through a lot. But we have to think about what we can do. To do nothing is not an option. Stephanie's life is in serious danger, and time is of the essence. You can relax awhile and get rested up, but we'll need you on the planning session. I suggest you go through the clothes in my sister's stateroom until you find what you need. Take a hot shower, a short rest. Those quarters are yours for the duration of the trip, so get comfortable in there. Oh, before you go, would you care to call your family?"

"No! I can't face that until I know what's happened to Stephanie. Wait, Mike. I remember hearing them say they're going to stay in the vicinity of Guadalupe Island and refuel from some kind of large ship. That had to be important."

"Thanks, Tracy. That's very important. Go on down. We have it for now."

Mike and Joel sat a few minutes before Joel spoke up. "We're only about twenty-five nautical miles from Guadalupe Island," Joel said. "I think we'd better stick close by until we get a handle on this thing."

"That's my thinking precisely, Joel. Set a reciprocal course taking us back to the island at about ten knots? We can lie in close to the northeast quarter of the island, put out a dive flag, and lower the small tender. We should drop the hook as close to shore as possible. That way, we give the appearance of continuing the dive pattern already established, ride out the rest of the daylight on anchor."

Mike looked away from the chart. "After dark, we cruise down the leeward side of the island, use the radar, stay well away from any cluster of vessels. Use the long-range radar to pick out targets we think might be that big sports fisher. Then we break out the high-intensity night-vision binoculars for a closer look."

After listening, Joel said, "You know I'm in agreement 100 percent on this caper, but it's my duty to point out that you have a hell of a lot to lose here. I don't want to be the bearer of bad news if things go really bad."

"That said, Joel, let's make things happen. We're still in Mexican waters. As insurance, we break out the hidden cache of emergency weapons."

"For sure, they're of no use to us hidden below decks, Mike."

"We already know how vicious our adversaries are, so we must be dedicated to success at all costs," Mike said. "It's self-defense first. The Mexican authorities aren't going to be helpful with this situation, only harmful to us, maybe more so than the narco crowd. They're connected at the hip."

Tracy followed Mike's instructions and went below into the most fabulous quarters she'd ever seen on a boat. Soft polished teakwood decor blended with the amazing quality of other furnishings. She kneeled near the big soft bed, placed elbows down, hands cupped beneath her chin. "Thank you, Lord, for the miracles of today, Lord, my life being a part of today's blessings. I'm sure you understand what I mean, Lord. This big unshaven person has returned into my life at a most unexpected and critical period of need. He may now have a family of his own, dear Lord, and if he does, I promise there'll be no interference on my part. I sense that he still has that once strong affection and passion that was evident so many years ago. Should such blessing be freely offered without encumbrances to this humble person, I'll accept with gratitude. Most important, Lord, bestow your blessings upon my sister, Stephanie, so that she may be released from the vicious persons who hold her prisoner. Save her life please, Lord, our Father in heaven."

After a shower and a brief rest, Tracy returned to the yacht's pilot house. She dressed in neat, clean blue jeans, a clean white T- shirt, and white boating shoes.

"Mike, I'm indebted to someone with exquisite taste for these comfortable clothes. I'll do my best to take care of them."

"My sisters would be pleased to have you share with them."

"Have I missed anything? Guys, I'm afraid you'll have to continue looking at this ugly puss a while longer. I tried makeup and then removed it again after realizing it only made me look more ridiculous."

Mike and Tracy stood alone in the large well-equipped ship's galley. Tracy looked at everything and opened one cabinet after the other. She reviewed the refrigerated foods, frozen foods and pastry selections, each in their own protective case. Mike reached across in front of Tracy, his arm touched the sensitive tip of a breast. Both aware of the effect, they looked at each other. Mike pulled Tracy to his chest and held her close. "I don't want to make you uncomfortable, Tracy, but I'm so pleased to have you here."

"I think I understand, Mike, but we don't really know each other anymore. We were frank and open with each other in that more innocent life, so young. I feel that I knew you well and trust in your integrity and good judgment. I see you have many of the same questions I have. Hold me for a few moments, please, and then let's help Stephie. I promise to be open and receptive to discuss our personal dilemma once we've helped my sister."

He released her, and she shifted her attention back to the chores at hand. "Mike, is it okay if I take over the galley duties? I want to help, not just take up space. I'll still be available to assist anywhere else as well. You go on up. I'll make lunch."

Tracy served a lunch of thick roasted beef sandwiches, potato chips, and cold beer. Afterward, they relaxed on the sundeck.

Blue Dolphin swung on anchor in the calm water near Guadalupe Island. Mike and Joel stretched out in the sun with only fishing shorts for protection from the tropical sun. Both men encouraged Tracy to don one of the several tiny bikini swimsuits available.

Tracy surprised them when she returned topside in a small blue bikini, matching her tan lines. Her full breasts overwhelmed the tiny bra top. Both Mike and Joel quickly offered to apply the necessary sunscreen.

Tracy laughed out loud in her well-remembered deep voice. Mike thought, *Thank God she still has it and spirit.*

She said, "Not today, guys," and slipped on sunglasses and a wide-brimmed hat. "You two need to concentrate on our rescue plan." She sat down in a reclining deck chair.

CHAPTER 9

Stephanie Conwell

June 16, 2015

"I've been thinking this thing through, Tracy. It's bigger than we could have imagined." Mike's analysis of the facts painted a dark picture for the girl held captive. *Any action is better than no action*, he thought, his give-no-quarter nature.

"We can't leave here without finding Stephanie, at least find that boat, her last known location. From this point on, we need to be alert for that sport fisher and any other vessel that looks suspicious. We'll remain here on anchor until we figure things out."

He put down his beer and ran fingers through his thick sun-bleached hair. "We're blessed with very calm conditions here on the lee side of the island. Joel and I need some rest, be sharp for tonight's work. Here's what we do."

Mike took off his cap and wiped his brow. "Starting now, Joel, you take the watch from the upper control station for about an hour. Tracy, you go down and get some rest. Take the second watch here on the bridge for an hour. Just report any boating activity at all to me. I'll take the third watch. By that time, we'll give the impression of visiting sport divers resting up at cocktail time. We'll hang here on anchor flying the dive flag, keeping a sharp eye out for that boat."

He turned down the volume on the emergency channel, then sat down again. "Now, listen. Here's how things stand. We're in Mexican waters, and that means no help from the authorities. We'll be acting just as much outside the law as the narco guys. We know they're vicious killers and will kill us all given the chance. Our only hope of success is stealth. Once they become aware of us as adversaries, we'll lose our advantage. We must agree on a plan, and then act fast, be quiet, and deadly aggressive. We're assuming the narco vessel remains in nearby waters, somewhere adjacent to Guadalupe Island. If that assumption is correct, then we have a slim chance of success."

He looked at Tracy. "Anything to add so far?"

She shook her head.

Mike continued, "Stephanie's only chance depends on our locating her whereabouts and taking aggressive action fast before the brothers do. If we stir up the hornet's nest too soon, without acting, there's very little chance of survival. Their vessel is likely nearby. They're not going to be cruising around burning up critical fuel. I think they'll be lying on anchor in an isolated bight, the lee side of Guadalupe Island."

Mike removed his long bib cap, massaged his temple firmly, and finished off his beer before continuing. "Joel, I'd like for you to go below into the lazarette shop after your watch and prepare two separate sections of anchor chain, each about four feet long. Do you suppose we can scrape up a couple of padlocks?"

"I think so, Mike. I'm sure we can confiscate a couple from the chests with the extra dive gear."

"That's good. While you're taking care of that, I'll lay out everything we need for cocktails and dinner in the upper salon. How would you like a big meal of grilled sea bass, grilled asparagus spears, and twice-baked potatoes? All left by the family. After that, we pick up the discussion and plan the evening's work."

Tracy said, "That sounds delicious, Mike, I'll help with that."

⌇⌇⌇

Joel looked hard at Mike. "So you plan on immobilizing that big vessel by wrapping a chain around each of the two props and locking them to the strut. That should do the job, all right. Now the difficult part! How do we get that heavy load to the vessel without being detected?"

"That's the tough part, all right, but here's what we have to do first. We must locate the vessel. Then we give those on board time to go down for the night, hoping they are confident enough to feel secure without an anchor watch. Tracy, have you handled a tender or small boat before?"

"I've driven outboards and a friend's inboard on water-skiing outings at Lake Mead. I can handle it, Mike."

"Okay. Once we've located and scouted the target, we'll use the smaller tender. We can attach the small electric trolling motor onto the transom next to the outboard. We have scuba equipment and night-vision gear onboard. If no one is on watch during the 2:00 to 3:00 AM period, we may not need the scuba gear. If we spot a night watch aboard, then we can have Tracy lay off at the necessary distance while we go underwater."

Mike took several deep swallows from the water bottle. "We wrap each short section of chain around a flotation device. Four feet of lightweight chain, like that used for the tenders or the stern anchors, won't sink a life vest. But when wrapped, it should compress the vest down to a smaller silhouette. Then we tow the bundle using thirty or forty feet of parachute cord from our shark fishing gear, secured with a snap fastener. If our luck holds and no watch is posted, then we motor close enough with the electric motor for Tracy to drop us in the shadow of the sport fisher. That way, Joel and I can push our load underneath the swim step. Once on board in bare feet and swim trunks, our best weapon will be the dive knife strapped to our leg."

He stopped for a moment. "Tracy, remember! Don't let the tender bump against the side of our target. A small sound on the outside is magnified on the inside and will wake the occupants. Now, tell us about the layout of this boat we have to board."

Tracy said, "All the cabins are up front. A large room is in front with two smaller rooms across from each other down the narrow hallway leading from the salon to the front cabin. If you enter from the swim step, go through the cockpit, straight on through the salon and galley, then down to the room on the right, where Stephanie should be. The men use the room on the left. There's a spiral staircase in the salon that leads to the flying bridge where the controls and radios are located. The upper bridge area is a large and comfortable room with a long seat in front of the helm."

She hesitated a moment. "I have a feeling that one of the men may be sleeping on that wide padded bench seat. I often took food and coffee up to the men. One of them was always stretched out on that seat and leaning against the window. I'm worried about Stephanie, guys. If you attempt to enter her room, she may scream and kick, waking up the other men. What should we do?"

"I know. That occurred to me as well. Ideas, Joel?"

"Yeah, here's the thing. We can't allow the guy on the bridge to get to the radio. A call out would ensure our destruction. So we must secure the bridge first."

"That means, at all costs, Joel. We can't be lucky enough to trap both men in the cabins below."

After a few moments, Mike said, "We should be moving soon if we hope to locate that boat. I'll set a course for the more protected south end of the island. We'll be using the long-range radar, staying well away from the shoreline. Then we can investigate each of the targets." Turning to Tracy, he said, "This is going to be a long night. Why don't you bring up the single-cup coffee maker and assorted mid-rations to keep us going tonight? When you get back, we'll continue our skull session. Meanwhile, I'll prepare the tender with everything we need for this phase of the operation."

Mike and Joel were talking when Tracy returned from her third trip below with enough K-Cups, pastries, and wrapped sandwiches for twice as many people.

Mike said, "It's time to move. Joel, pull the stern anchor and prepare to get underway as planned." Mike passed a full cup of coffee to Tracy. "Once we step onto the swim step, Tracy, you back off a safe distance. We've agreed that I'll secure the bridge. Joel's going to stand by in the passage-way between the two cabins. If and when I get the bridge secured without a lot of noise, Joel will hold his position, and I'll let you know when to come around to the swim step where I'll tie off the tender."

Moonlight reflected all around the nearby island. Joel said, "Moving in closer was a good idea. We've cruised for two hours, and the best prospect was about five miles back, that large white boat glaring in the moonlight."

Mike said, "Cruise around the south end at a leisurely pace of ten knots, Joel, then return past the suspect boat. None of the other radar silhouettes are large enough, and they don't fit the profile. Make the return at about two hundred yards from shore. We can get a good picture of every-thing on the way back. That won't attract attention. I think it wise to make a midnight surveillance run with the large tender. Okay, Joel, let's have Tracy flip a coin to see which of us takes the first turn in the barrel." Fishing for a coin, Mike said, "Here, Tracy, my lucky quarter. I take heads."

Joel said, "I don't trust either of you, but go ahead and flip it."

Tracy calls out, "Heads." Then she said, "Oh, shit, Mike, let me go with you. Please." She looked at him, ready to beg if necessary.

Joel said, "I told you so."

After a moment of thought, Mike looked at Tracy. "Okay. You're a big part of this operation from beginning to end. Joel, it's nearly 1:00 AM. I think I recall a small headland about a mile past what looks like our target. That should shield Blue Dolphin from a radar silhouette. Put out at least an eight-to-one scope to hold us in place. Use the heavier starboard anchor. I'm going out on the boat deck and switch the electric motor over to the larger tender. Just in case of trouble, I want a nine-millimeter under the helm of each tender before we launch. Let's hope we don't need to use them."

He looked at Tracy. "Go down and find yourself a dark pullover long-sleeved shirt. Don't want it too heavy in case we take to the water, but it'll get cold on the tender, speeding across the water this time of night."

Joel said, "The anchor is well set, launch the RIB, Mike. So you know, we're anchored just at the outer tip of the headland. Our radar silhouette will blend with the island yet allow me to watch you on radar. Just don't get caught. You can use the tender radio if necessary. It's set on channel 12. I'll monitor it, with plenty of others. You guys be careful and come back home to Papa with all the right answers."

The four-stroke outboard started at once. Mike engaged the drive gear and moved away. He turned to Tracy. "Move to the rear and locate the electric control switch on the small electric motor next to the big motor." He'd explained the use prior to launching. "Go ahead, Tracy, you have control. I'll kill the big engine."

Tracy moved the control to a slow setting and maneuvered the craft from side to side, increasing speed. "It's so quiet. I only hear movement of water," she said.

"Okay, any more questions?"

"No. Now, let me start the bigger motor."

"Okay, kid. Get over here beneath the wheel."

Tracy grabbed the wheel, reached for the ignition key, and turned the key to start. Nothing happened. She looked at Mike.

"Move the shifter to neutral. The starter won't engage unless it's in neutral," he said.

"Gotcha." Tracy moved the shifter back and forth a few times and found the neutral position. The engine started. She engaged the gear and moved off. After a few sharp back-and-forth turns, she returned control to Mike. He and Tracy headed south and hugged the coastline.

Mike said, "Stop! A large boat outlined against the night sky. That's it. There can't be more than one big customized sports fisher like that within five hundred miles." He passed the light-sensitive binoculars to Tracy. "Tell me what you think."

"That does look like the boat. I remember those two big tanks on top of that arch thing with all those antennas."

Mike explained, "You're looking at satellite navigation and telephone equipment. Hold us here near the shore. I want'a study this thing with the night-vision equipment."

After fifteen or twenty minutes of careful observation, Mike removed the night-vision headset and placed the harness over Tracy's head. "Move this little lever up and down for focus."

Tracy adjusted the lever back and forth a little. "This is fantastic. It's eerie with that bright-yellow glow all over things. I can see it all much better. It's almost like just before dawn breaks."

"Okay, hurry now. Let me have the headset. It's time to go before someone pops up to take a look around. The current is carrying us in their direction."

CHAPTER 10

Attack at Zero Dark Thirty

June 17, 2015

"We have no choice here. *Blue Dolphin* has to be left on anchor with no one onboard," Mike said. "Tracy, are you sure about your part in this scheme?"

They crowded into the small tender. "Yes, Mike! My safety's not an issue, you know that."

"Okay then, we want to get Stephie into the tender with you soon as she's free. Lay off away from the boat fifty feet or so and wait for Joel and me. If you hear gunfire, move even farther away, and wait for us to call you by name. You'll know it's time to use the gun under the helm, if the brothers show up outside without us. Joel, can you think of anything else before we shove off?"

"No, the *Dolphin* is well hooked. Let's see what we can do about those guys holding Stephanie."

With Tracy at the controls, they approached with caution, within one hundred feet of the large vessel. A breeze rippled the water, and a soft slapping sound came from the larger vessel.

Mike saw no one on watch and whispered to Tracy, "Hold it right here. No sign of a night watch. Once we're out, move into the shadow near shore until we signal you to come in close."

Mike and Joel are dressed in dark fishing shorts, fins, and dive masks for the swim. "Don't need the cord, Joel. Let the flotation devices float away after we reach our target. There'll be some rattling of the chain. Work slow. It'll be mistaken for anchor chain dragging over the rocky bottom. You secure the port propeller first, while I watch for any activity onboard. Once the portside propeller is secured, climb into the cockpit with your knife ready while I secure the starboard propeller."

Both propellers were locked tight with a minimum amount of noise. Mike eased onto the swim step, kicked off his fins, and stepped into the cockpit. Joel slipped down into the lower passageway, where sleeping quarters were located. Mike watched in the dim light as Joel wedged the blade of his heavy dive knife into the wall behind the sliding door of the small stateroom on the left, securing it temporarily.

Mike climbed the spiral ladder to the enclosed flying bridge. He saw no one, heard a groan, saw a man sit up on the padded bench seat, and rubbed his eyes. Mike moved fast and reached for the man's hands to wrap them with duct tape. The man shouted out and slammed both feet into Mike's midsection, forcing him back near the stairs. He recovered, faced his attacker, deflected the blow, and sent a hard right to the face. The man tumbled backward down the steel ladder and bounced out onto the deck below. Mike dropped down to the man on the deck and bound both hands in front with duct tape.

The second man cursed in Spanish and attempted to break down the door where he was trapped. Joel had all his weight pressed against the strong knife jammed into the wall and prevented the sliding door from opening. He shouted, "What do we do now, Mike?"

"On my signal, retrieve your knife and step back to your right. That'll put his momentum toward me. Watch for any kind of weapon."

The door flew open, and the man rushed toward Mike, slashing wildly. Mike delivered another lightning blow at the man's face. Mike's hard fist glanced off the chin into the exposed throat, crushing the larynx. He dropped to his knees and struggled for breath.

Joel reached for the struggling man's hands. Mike touched his shoulder. "Don't bother. I don't think he'll make it."

Joel saw blood dripping, an open wound. "Look at you! Are you okay to keep going?"

Mike looked down at a long cut across his right hip just below the beltline, a ten-inch gash. His fishing shorts were sliced open, hanging loose. He saw it was shallow, bleeding. "Yeah, check to be sure we're alone, then tie the tender to the swim step. Ask Tracy to come aboard. I'll find the key for the other room." Mike listened at the door and felt better at once. He detected a tearful feminine cough.

Mike turned his full attention back to the assailant struggling for one last breath before falling on his side. He noticed a ring of keys clipped to the man's belt. He felt for a carotid artery, detected no pulse, then released the snap ring holding the keys to the belt.

Joel checked the master's suite, then moved on to check the other assailant at the bottom of the stairs duct-taped earlier by Mike. He detected no pulse or breath. Joel was now confident they were alone. He walked outside and waved Tracy over.

Tracy maneuvered the tender alongside and waited for Joel to secure it to the swim platform.

Joel spoke in a calm voice. "Everything's good. We believe Stephanie's in her cabin where you thought she'd be. I think Mike may be injured. He isn't letting on about it, but he may be losing blood. You help him free your sister while I look for a first-aid kit. All vessels of this size have something to serve that purpose."

Mike switched on the lights in the hallway and located the proper key to unlock the room Stephanie was believed to be in. He waited for Tracy to arrive before unlocking and opening the door, then looked down at the bloody gash across his hip. Blood soaked through the fishing shorts and ran down his leg onto his bare foot. The bleeding appeared to have slowed. His brain worked fast. He analyzed the situation and decided on a course of action in light of what just happened.

Tracy rushed through to Mike. "Are you all right?" The dim light in the passageway was enough to make the scene appear bad. She looked down at Mike's bloody leg, ignored the man curled up on the floor, reached for Mike, and buried her face against his chest.

"I'm okay. We have to release Stephanie and see if she's injured. Are you ready?"

She stared at the long gash above the bloody leg and foot and moved her head up and down. "What do we do?"

"Stand back until we're sure there's no surprise waiting for us in there." Mike unlocked the door and eased it back to get a look into the dark room. There's just enough light for him to see a small frame curled up with a pillow, making a quiet sniffling sound. He stepped aside and gestured for Tracy to go in, pointing at the figure on one of the two beds.

Tracy whispered, "Steph, it's me," and touched her shoulder. Stephanie looked around and grabbed Tracy around the neck, pulling her all the way over onto the bed.

"Oh god, oh god, oh god." Both women cried, clinging to each other.

Mike said, "Look, girls, it's late, and we still have work to do. Come outside. He led the way past the man in the salon and out into the cockpit. Are you okay, Stephanie?"

Stephanie tipped her head and looked at Mike and Joel. "Thank you both so much. I don't know who you are, but it has to be a miracle. I thought for sure that Tracy was gone. Hondo and Duck said she jumped overboard with her hands tied."

Mike spoke up and nudged the girls forward toward Joel. "We can catch up with everything once aboard *Blue Dolphin*. We're going to be running out of darkness. Joel! Take the girls to the boat and hurry back. We have to search this thing and prepare it for our departure."

Mike checked the man who fell down the staircase into the salon. As suspected, he didn't regain consciousness from the fall. He paused. Two dead people. It's just as well. We have nothing to lose now by covering our tracks.

Mike moved to the main salon and searched it well. So far he'd located two separate hideaways—the first, in the center of the king-size bed, underneath the mattress. A light-gauge metal box with locked lid mounted in the wooden frame and covered over with a simple thin throw rug. None of the keys from the ring fit the lock but would be simple to breach with the right tool. The second hideaway, a large open space behind a full-size hinged mirror on the starboard bulkhead. He found a row of ladies' handbags on one of the shelves. Mike felt sure the girls would be able to iden-tify their own among the many. Next, he checked the large shower and toilet facility, including a small dressing table and mirror inside the enclosure. He found nothing unusual there. He entered the larger room where the two brothers kept their belongings while on board. Here he found two per-sonal wallets for the brothers with their identifications and a small amount of cash. He looked into one of two hanging lockers and picked up a dark blue canvass bag. He opened the heavy bag, astonished at the bundles of cash, mostly $50 or $100 bills, in US currency.

Joel entered the salon where Mike was sitting, stunned by what he'd found.

Mike explained, "This stash has to be the brothers' expense money or money to pay associates."

Joel was amazed, then noticed Mike's wound again. "Let's take a minute to clean up that gash on your leg. Otherwise, it might get infected." Joel cleaned the wound and put a temporary bandage over the long cut across Mike's hip.

"Joel, I hope you agree with me. Our best option is to leave no sign of our presence. We need to scuttle this boat, send the whole thing down where the water is deep enough to hide what happened here from the cartel. She's hooked on the edge of the cliff right now. We can let out another few hundred feet of chain on this beauty and use the tender to tow her off to the east where the depth drops off fast. With the props locked up like they are, it may be a simple matter of revving those large engines and placing it in gear. Something has to give. Either the struts will rip loose, or the engines will break loose from the engine mounts, ripping loose the saltwater intake."

Joel said, "To begin with, let me find something to pry open that metal locker in the bed." In short order, he returned from the tool locker with a medium-sized pry bar. "This should do the job." It took only minutes to open the box where they found more hard cash. The locker was deeper than expected. "We can't leave this filthy stuff in here to pollute the water, can we?"

Mike reached in the closet for another canvas bag. It was full of clothes. He emptied out the bag, handed it to Joel who began filling it with the cash. "One should be enough, don't you think? We have to hurry and get loaded up, need this trunk on the bottom before daylight, if possible."

Loading everything into the tender, Joel said, "Let's slash the intake hoses first to be sure. Then we'll open deck hatches in the cockpit and cut off electricity to the bilge pumps. Flip to see who starts up the engines." He flipped the coin, then grinned at Mike. "You lose, big guy. I get the honors. I'll join you in a jiffy."

They moved around the boat and got her ready for the dive. Mike tied a towline to the tender. Joel started up the engines, engaged both transmissions, opened the throttle on both big diesels, and raced to the railing. He looked around fast and slipped under the railing, lowering himself down into the tender.

Mike gunned the throttle. The 90 horsepower outboard had no problem swinging the stern of the big boat out to deeper water. "Listen to that!" A loud screaming noise came from the stressed transmissions. Another ripping, banging noise also filled the air when one and then the other rear struts securing the propeller shaft to the boat hull broke away flinging the heavy chain around. Water rushed in and filled the rear cavity of the vessel. The open hatch above where the strut was fastened to the hull had water spraying three feet high. The anchor chain stretched out tight.

Mike said, "That's it. The stern quarter is dipping under. Cast off the line, and let's head home."

Joel scanned the skies and horizon before commenting. "Lucky for us there've been no signs of aircraft or other boating activity in the area since yesterday afternoon. Hey, look! The engines are still racing as she goes below the surface. There must be an air pocket in the engine room."

The sky grew lighter. Mike looked at *Blue Dolphin* and saw the women looking their way. Both rushed down. Tracy said, "Is everything okay, Mike? We were getting concerned."

"Thanks, Tracy. It all went well. I hope you girls have rested and had something to eat and drink. We're bushed."

Relief's obvious on Tracy's face. "You ladies, please get settled in for a good six to eight hours' rest," Mike said. *We have a lot to talk about, but it can wait. There's a long voyage ahead, and we may each be assigned a standby watch while we're at sea.*

He sat down and looked at Joel. "We should clear this area now without obvious haste. At best, the sun will be up before we clear the northern tip of the island. Check the weather first, and let's get underway on course zero degrees magnetic. We have about four hundred miles of open sea ahead. I'm concerned about a chance encounter with one of the cartel's large host vessels that the Guerrero brothers were in communication with. That guy Lance may have checked us out, identified the *Dolphin*, and spread the word."

Joel said, "I'll take care of the tenders and get us seaworthy. You don't look too good, Mike."

Tracy said, "We have to deal with that injury first, Mike. It really needs stitches."

Mike acknowledged, "Do that for me, please. Just clean it up for the time being."

Mike returned. "I'll get us moving, Joel. Before the girls turn in, can you help them report in with their parents or other family? Would you mind doing that? I think I need to stay in the background until I hear more of the facts from Tracy. She's being closemouthed about her personal life."

CHAPTER 11

Port San Quentin

June 11–18, 2015

Dr. Figueroa said, "Lance, you're leaving the hospital too soon. I've done everything I can for you. Follow my instructions, keep the stitching clean, dry, and continue treating with antibiotic cream, or you'll have noticeable scarring on your face. The broken ribs will also give you more trouble than you expect without proper treatment. I advise you to stay here a couple of days more to be on the safe side."

"No, Doc! I'm trying to run a business. I've got a lot in play right now. Got to get back to work. You sign the damn release slip. I'm out of here."

"You paid for my service. Now take my advice. Limit your activity for the next few weeks."

Lance felt the blast of humid air outside. Son of a bitch! He damned all big muscle-bound assholes as well as the weather and half of the other people he knew.

"August, what'd you find out about the bastard that blindsided me in the toilet?"

"I've got several people working on it. You're going to need patience on this. We haven't got much to go on. Word is he had to be a truck driver operating in and out of the port there in Cabo. He fit the description of several big men operating from California or Arizona. Forget about that guy for now, Lance. He'll show up again, and then we'll get him."

"Fuck you, August, not your face the bastard busted up. I've got it all set up with my guys. Once we locate him, I'll cut him up good."

"Frankly, I don't trust the Guerreros to handle things around Guadalupe, Chief. This is one of the largest deliveries we've ever organized, and we should concentrate on getting it finalized before something or someone screws it up."

"You're right, of course. Those two turds grabbed my personal yacht and a pot full of cash. One more thing, August, they've got two of the best-looking women I've ever seen locked up on board waiting for me to work out a deal through our Middle Eastern brokers. Those babes should bring a record-breaking price. Now, let's get home so we can keep tabs on the Guerrero boys. They had better not screw this thing up."

Augustine rushed into Lance's air-conditioned office above the warehouse floor. "One of the ferry captains just came in. He said he was present aboard your yacht last night for the transfer of funds. It appeared to have gone anyway, but good. Furthermore, some of the shipping people are hesitant to do more business until final payment for this deal is made. They're demanding your presence on any future business. Would you care to fill me in?"

"The fucking ship's captain demanded an extra hundred grand for himself at the rendezvous. I ordered the Guerrero brothers to deliver only 50 percent of what's owed until the ship's owners can be contacted. Those were my instructions, August."

Lance stood and scratched his crotch. "Some of the boys are getting greedy. We can't let them think we're losing control, or things will get out of hand. The Guerrero boys have another meeting on the 17th for final payment. They're to return here immediately after the meeting. They also have the full half million in cash on board. No one else is aware of that, August. Let's hope it stays that way."

———～～～———

Seated in front of an array of high-tech satellite communications equipment in Lance's office, later in the day, both men are visibly upset.

"My last conversation with Hondo was at eleven thirty last night," Lance said. "Everything was on schedule for an afternoon meeting confirmed with the ship's representative for two thirty this afternoon. The asshole was supposed to call me at eight sharp this morning to check in. I've called the yacht every thirty minutes since then and still get no response. We don't have any other boats in the area, do we?"

"No. Port San Quentin is the closest mainland seaport within range. We don't have another load planned from here until July 22. The long-range trawlers are fishing south of here during downtime."

"I've a bad feeling about this. There's too much at stake here," Lance said.

"Remember, Lance, they could've been tempted by the half million in cash. It makes me think we've been taken. You think you should put out an alert for your yacht?"

"Damn it to hell, August. Our only help here is going to come from our own initiative and our own people. Get in touch with the trawler skippers and see what they know."

Still fuming, he said, "Here's what I want you to do after that. Get out to the nearest airport that offers charters and hire something with enough range to search the area around Guadalupe Island first. If they were there at nine thirty last night, then a plane search will locate the bastards. You know what? I don't know for sure that's where they were at that time. If they planned to take the money and run, they had time to get almost anywhere. Hell, we don't know for sure that something's wrong. Shit! We don't know anything, do we?"

"Well, boss, I still think it's a good bet that we start looking now. We can cancel everything quickly if you hear from them. I never trusted those two anyway."

"Stay in touch, August. I'll call you if I reach them. Meanwhile, I'm alerting all of our contacts here and in the US to be on the lookout for *Sly Fox* and the Guerrero brothers." I'm not about to let August or anyone else know there's over a million dollars of my own money hidden aboard the *Sly Fox* on top of the half million owed to the shipping outfit.

Augustine returned to Lance's office from the cubby hole down in the warehouse where he conducts his cartel business. "Lance, I've exhausted all possibilities except one. There's an expatriate American in La Paz who has a twin engine Seneca with a five-hundred-mile range. This guy's name is Mark Wynn, and the airplane is in San Jose Viejo today. He'll be back in La Paz tomorrow morning. The earliest he can be airborne is 11:00 AM tomorrow, the 18th. He's asking for a $5,000 deposit up front to take off."

"Okay, August, I can't take to the air myself, so you go along and stay in touch with me here at the office. I don't plan to leave until this situation is worked out. I've been in touch with the ship's representative, and I'll know for sure about the Guerrero boys by this afternoon at rendezvous time. I'll let you know then. It was necessary to guarantee full payment to the owners regardless of today's outcome. The situation with the captain will be taken care of by their organization."

He grabbed Augustine's arm. "August, I'm giving you enough cash to keep that plane in the air until we locate the

Sly Fox. You know how we operate, so I'll need an accounting of every dollar. Get that plane in the air as soon as you can tomorrow. We know there's a good chance those guys planned to run with the cash right after the first meeting on June 14th. If that's true, then they could be as far as one thousand miles from the rendezvous point at Guadalupe Island. Start your air search from La Paz down around the shoreline to Cabo and up, checking all potential ports of call where fuel and supplies could be purchased. At Isla Cerros, fly directly out to Guadalupe and take a close look at all the coves where *Sly Fox* could be hiding."

Augustine stopped Lance. "This is going to be time-consuming. Couldn't it wait?"

"Hell no! Return to the mainland and continue north all the way to the border area, but don't forget to look around any of the offshore islands such as the Coronado's. Work with the pilot as necessary to plan your fuel stops. I seriously doubt that they'd cross the border into the US. If we don't locate the *Sly Fox* with this air search, then I'm afraid that the escape plan may have taken them across to Mazatlán. I plan to alert our contacts as far south as Guatemala."

～～～

Those thieving bastards have stolen my boat, found my personal funds in the bed, and run. The value of the boat and cash aboard, nearly three million dollars lost—enough to tempt Father Murphy himself. Got to find that boat.

Lance was dangerous to be around. Workers preparing the next shipment avoided him. He turned from his desk, kicked the trash can across the room, and called Maria from her desk outside. "Get Capitan Mendez in here as soon as he's back in port. My best man flying all over Mexico instead of directing the workers and stockpiling product at the warehouse."

Lance leaned over his desk and agonized over the last few days. *Everything was going fine until that big bastard interfered. I'm going to kill him, but first, he has to know who I am and suffer ten times as much pain as he caused me. It's his fault this shipment is in jeopardy.*

Lance looked at his watch and realized time was short. Better get the operation back on track. He picked up the phone and dialed a number. "Augustine, this is Lance. Call me when you're back on the ground."

CHAPTER 12

Reap the Spoils of War

June 17, 2015

Aboard *Blue Dolphin*, Tracy and Stephanie waited, attempted to rest, and failed. "I panicked, Stephanie! Thought that island was close enough I could swim right to it. I swam for an hour. It seemed farther away. I realized my strength was going and tried to rest for a moment on the kelp bed. I looked up. A huge unshaven man seemed to appear out of the sea itself. I thought it was a trick of the mind, was so tired. My eyes got blurry."

She wiped away a tear, and continued. "Mike was so gracious, didn't hesitate, wanted to find you. He's unaware of my deep secret, sis. I feel so guilty not sharing with him years ago." She accepted a hand full of tissue from Stephanie.

"Here, Tracy, catch." Joel heaved a large heavy plastic bag onto the deck at her feet.

"This is for you, Stephanie." He placed a small neat travel case near her.

Stephanie squealed with delight. "That's my travel case! I thought it was gone forever. Thanks, Joel!"

Joel stored the two canvas bags in the dive compartment and returned to steady up the tenders for open sea.

Tracy opened the plastic bag, looked inside, and dumped everything out onto the deck. "Look, Steph, here's my purse." She grabbed it, looked through it fast, pulled out a phone then her wallet, and checked to be sure her credit cards and identification were intact. "Wheeeee! What a relief. What purse did you have, Steph?"

Stephanie closed her travel case and turned to look at Tracy and the many handbags scattered there on the carpeted salon. "There! That one over there." She pointed at a large stylish bag near Tracy. Stephanie stepped around the scattered bags and picked up the one indicated, knowing at once that it was her missing handbag.

"This is my bag, Tracy. That lowlife bastard had our bags all along. You suppose these other handbags belong to more missing women?"

"Stephanie, it's time you and I opened our eyes. This kind of evil is so close to us, the people we mingle with. I would never expect normal-looking people like that jerk Lance to be capable of such brutality. Let's face it. You and I are fortunate to be alive and here to talk about it. The women who lost those bags may have lost their lives."

Tracy sat next to Mike and waited to get his attention.

Mike said, "Joel? Do you feel like handling the bridge? I need about an hour, and then you can take an eight-hour rest. You won't have to be on deck again until four this afternoon."

Tracy said, "Mike, you need to do something about that injury. Get it cleaned and taped together."

Mike nodded.

Joel said, "I can handle things here, Mike. You take the time you need. I'll keep us on our course, due north, into San Diego, right?"

"That's it, Joel, the latest weather report indicates we'll have uncommonly good weather for the next three hundred miles, then it'll get rough. We could have some problems with a pressure gradient predicted off Southern California."

Tracy watched Mike sag into one of the raised command chairs before continuing. She admired his stamina.

Joel said, "We'll take our time for the next thirty-six hours. It's possible we'll miss the worst of those winds."

"A good chance of that. We should have about three hundred miles of decent weather. She's in your hands, Joel. I'll see you here in about an hour."

Mike turned to Tracy. "Why don't you get Stephanie settled in your cabin then give me a hand? I'll be in D suite, getting cleaned up. Each stateroom has a medical kit. Just come in when you can."

Tracy knocked and entered the room. Mike sat in a comfortable chair, drying his blond hair with a large towel. He'd dressed in a clean white T-shirt and boxer shorts. His trim physique didn't go unnoticed by Tracy. Still unsure about things, she hesitated and gained control. *Old feelings die hard*, she thought. "Mike, you lovable miscreant. I can't stand much of this."

"I know, Tracy. We have to talk. I'm going crazy not knowing everything about you and your family. You can't know how I fantasized about a miraculous reunion. Never dreamed it'd be like this."

"It's not fair for you to say such things, Mike. You must have a beautiful family of your own by now after all these years."

"Never found the right one after you. I looked at every woman I went out with and hoped to find some of you hiding in there. My father once accused me of acting like a blind dung beetle running around, looking for a hole in a concrete pasture. He may have been right, because I'm still looking for that special something or someone that I once found, only to lose way too soon."

"Are you telling me now that you've never been married? You . . . a successful attractive man?"

"That's right, Tracy. I'm still hoping for that family, searching for the right partner. Now, tell me all about you, the beautiful young athletic mother-in-waiting that I remember."

"If you must know, Mike, she's still waiting for the father of her children. That's all you need to know for now. We're all tired, and you don't want to keep Joel on hold. He's as tired as any of us. Let me help you dress your injured hip. Does this kit have all we need?"

"Yes. I cleaned the gash well with soap and water, but it's difficult to reach for proper care. I'll lie on my side so you can get to it. You can pull my pants down without my help," he said, a huge smile on his face.

"You're still the frisky young Turk I remember. Maybe I should've stayed on that kelp bed." She grabbed his shorts and yanked them down past his shiny white ass.

Tracy returned to the bridge, rested on the couch behind Joel, and dozed off.

Joel touched Tracy's shoulder. "You looked so tired, hated to wake you. The sleeping troll wanted an hour of rest. He's had more than two. Want to do the honors?"

Somewhat refreshed, she went down to where Mike was sleeping, woke him with a soft kiss, and returned to the bridge.

Tracy relaxed in the second command chair and watched Mike do his thing. He appeared rested, explained what he was doing, stayed busy, double-checked their course, projected fuel usage, and tracked a large radar target. She guessed it to be a car carrier or other large ship. He showed her some instruments pertaining to the ship's mechanical and electrical systems. They appeared to be performing as they should. During slack periods, he began planning a few good meals with her. She felt tired and went down to freshen up.

At two forty-five in the afternoon, Tracy joined Mike on the bridge again. She was dressed in tan shorts and a white halter top that left a narrow white strip of untanned breast exposed. He noticed. She couldn't resist, stood on her toes, and placed a tender kiss to the corner of his mouth.

He smiled and looked at Tracy's green eyes. "You know you shouldn't do this to me."

Tracy laughed with her deep-throated resonance. "I'm just offering to help with the chores. By the way, Steph asked about using the washer and dryer later today."

"Yeah, that's fine. I'm sure you'll find what you need in the laundry area. What do you think about you and me preparing a nice meal to serve here in the upper salon about four? It'd be a pleasant surprise for the others."

"That's a wonderful idea, Mike. It'll also make me feel useful. Stephanie is out cold, sleeping in that air-conditioned room."

Mike picked up a yellow notepad and handed it to Tracy. "Here, look this over. Just ideas for meals. I'd like to see us all have two good meals a day. We can snack or drink beer the rest of the time. As of now, that responsibility is yours and Steph's. Okay?"

"You got it, Mike! We'll take it from here. How about using that drop leaf in the salon for the main meals? I'm going down, Mike, to get familiar with what's available from the galley and food storage lockers. Can I bring you anything?"

"I could use a beer, been on a coffee diet for more than six hours."

She looked at him, had a sudden urge to hug him, then resisted.

Throughout the day, the blue ocean remained smooth and calm. Tracy relaxed on the open deck with binoculars in one hand, a cold Corona in the other, until a clean-shaven Joel joined her.

"Hi, Joel, you look much more rested. Can I get you anything from below? It makes me feel useful and keeps my legs from getting flabby." Before he could answer, she pointed. "Look! I can't believe the huge school of porpoise. They're everywhere."

Joel said, "Have you ever watched them from the bow? You get a different look as they jump the bow wake, swim in and out, from underneath the boat."

"That sounds like fun. Is it safe out there?"

"Oh, yeah, as long as you don't lean out over the railing too far."

Joel opened the door. A strong breeze blew through. "Go on out, but hold the railing. After we get a look at the action, I'll help you with all that food you've prepared."

Stephanie looked out at the spectacle and saw Joel. He waved her forward.

"Come out with us, Stephanie. You'll see an interesting close-up of nature at its best. Just be careful. Sometimes the boat will take an unexpected roll, so keep one hand tight on the railing as you move forward." The warm breeze whipped through the girls' hair as they stepped outside.

Tracy's long hair covered her face. Stephanie said, "Oh God, look down, Tracy. They're racing with us. I think that one's looking at us. Look how big his eyes are."

Joel encouraged them to step to the bow for a different feeling as the ship rose and fell with the ocean swell. He looked back at the bridge. "Okay, girls, enough. Let's see if we can feed the hungry captain. He looks dead on his feet."

Tracy looked at Mike slumped back in the captain's chair. The enclosed bridge, separated from the salon by a plate glass window and wet bar, allowed him to watch the activity at both ends of the ship. She knew he longed for a little rest, caught Joel's eye, and suggested feeding him.

"How's it shaping up out there, Pard?" Mike said.

"Everything's good so far. That's some feast the girls have laid out. I checked below decks before coming up. You should consider yourself relieved and get stoked up for a good rest, tired old friend. I can keep one eye on everything here while we grab a bite, looks delicious."

"That's good, Joel. Can you handle things until midnight? Maybe set the girls up with a two-hour relief watch during the middle of our eight hours. It'll keep us awake and provide a pee break. Of course, one of us will always be sacked out here in the sea cabin. I'm dead tired, so it's up to you to brief them on everything."

Tracy grabbed his arm. "Come on, sad sack, you need nourishment and a good rest."

Joel said, "I've got the bridge. Go on and grab a bite."

"Got a lot on my mind," Mike said. "We need to put our heads together and figure out what should be done about the two canvas bags and how we handle the unavoidable check-in with the authorities in San Diego."

Tracy pushed him toward where a delightful meal was set out.

Mike said, "Hi, Stephanie. You're beautiful! How did you do it?"

She hugged him. "You're just a big sweet talker, Mike. Besides, Tracy has always been the beauty of our family."

Tracy felt anxious. "Mike, I'm having trouble forgetting Hondo's body lying there on the deck. And then there was Duck. I'm concerned about you and Joel being in trouble, nothing more. Are you going to have a serious problem with

it? Those two were violent predators and deserved everything that happened to them."

He said, "Listen to me. This may upset you more, but
everything will be okay. I'm tired right now and may not be
thinking straight, but here's what we have to deal with. First,
there's the matter of the unavoidable death of two members
of a violent drug cartel, as you pointed out. Next, there's the
uncertainty of not knowing if we've been identified by Lance
Howell, a leader with this violent cartel. Third, it was necessary to dispose of a million-dollar vessel to prevent any
association or connection to those of us here, with those
violent deaths." He looked at her before continuing.

"I know, Mike. I'm trying to process it all."

"And fourth, there's something that may make it easier
to swallow. It's possible. You may have become wealthy as
a result of your ordeal."

She puzzled over his statement and opened her mouth
to speak.

"Hold on, and I'll explain in a moment. Fifth, and most
important, we must present a plausible story to the authorities as we check back into the United States. Our story will
be looked at with care, because we need to turn over those
recovered handbags. That's something, my dear, that needs
to be investigated. As for the death of two violent killers, my
conscience doesn't bother me at all. And for the possibility of wealth . . . Joel? Would you mind bringing up those
two canvas bags? Now, Tracy, we're all in this predicament
together. There's a great deal of money in those bags Joel's
bringing up. You and Stephanie should take it someplace
quiet, maybe into the unused dining room, and count it. I
believe that the cash is in bundles. If so, note the denomina-
tions, then count each bundle to ensure accuracy."

She's confused, even more worried now. "Mike, I don't
understand. Doesn't this just complicate the problem?"

"Maybe not, it has to be handled in a proper manner."

She could tell he's patient, trying to explain everything for her. "I'm only concerned about you getting in serious trouble. You've done so much for Steph and me."

"I don't want to say 'Trust me' and then disappoint you, but it will work out. Let me handle things. I'm sorry if all this makes you more uncertain. Now, on the money, make a notation on one sheet of paper only. We don't want any kind of evidence left around to create questions. I'm going down and try to sleep for six or seven hours. If I don't get some rest, that mid watch is going to be hell on water."

"I don't know what to say, Mike. Nothing like this could be happening to us. Stephanie and I are ordinary boring people. Won't all that money just complicate our problem more?"

CHAPTER 13

Zero Degrees North

June 17, 2015

Tracy watched Joel thumb back through the boat's logbook. He found what he was looking for and marked it with a sticky note. They talked about the money. She attempted to draw information from Joel about Mike's job, his family, and anything else she could get. Joel spoke well of Mike and the close family corporation up to a point, then deferred to Mike for answers. After a while, he decided to share Mike's log entry with her. She saw him open the book at a marked point.

"I'm going to read Mike's log entry to you," Joel said. "It's entered on the date of departure from Cabo San Lucas, June 10th, including a tempered version of the abuse of two women inside the *Naked Mermaid*. Mike plans to cover this with you himself."

"A desperate request for assistance from the two women followed an encounter near an old van outside the restaurant. The women appeared to be under distress, asked for help, and accepted an offer of sanctuary aboard this vessel at the Hotel Baha Marina."

Farther along in the log, Joel read another entry. "While cruising near a small debris field off the Isle of Guadalupe, we observed a large white plastic bag that was retrieved for proper disposal. It felt unusual. Upon examination, we discovered nine women's purses containing various identification papers of US citizens."

Tracy stopped him there. "So that's how we explain it."

Joel said, "If there's an answer to the problem, Mike, the most resourceful person he'd ever known, would find it. As far as the money, neither he nor Mike was excited about it, but would have been plain stupid to leave it behind. Something practical would be worked out."

―――〜〜〜―――

Joel dumped the two heavy canvas bags onto the teakwood dining table. Tracy and Stephanie stepped up to look inside. The smaller of the two bags was opened first. Tracy looked at the thick bricks of currency, all packed in tight with the green side up.

"Are we dreaming, Steph? Does this mean we share in all of this money? I'm afraid to touch it. I might wake up back in the ocean, struggling to keep my face out of the water."

"This is no dream, Tracy. I've never met a man like Mike. Why didn't you talk about him years ago? You told me about someone but refused to elaborate, even under duress. And you did have plenty of that."

"At that time in my life, Steph, I was prideful and independent and believed I was self-sufficient. I also knew what I was in for when I allowed myself to fall deep in love after the best three days of my life. Please don't tell Mike anything about my life since then. I promise, I'll tell him before this trip is over. He deserves it. I thought until a few days ago I was over the emotions. Even at this minute, after so long, I still want to curl up in his arms and cry my heart out."

Tracy changed her focus back to the canvas bags. "Now, can we count the money?"

After counting and taking notes for two hours, Tracy and Steph joined Joel on the bridge.

"Thanks, Joel. That was very enlightening. Now for a few winks on the sofa before we go for the bear."

The pillows stored beneath the couch were small but soft and smooth. She looked through the selection of blankets and spread one over Steph, who was already curled up asleep.

At 11:00 PM sharp, Tracy was awakened by a touch on her shoulder. "It's time to wake the sleeping giant. Would you like to do the honors?" Joel said.

"Of course, may I take a couple of private minutes first?"

"Sure, you might also see what's available for a midnight snack. Otherwise, he'll stick with a coffee diet all night."

Tracy tapped on Suite D, left the door open for light, and gazed down at the sleeping man. She was always fascinated by Mike's large masculine, less-than-perfect face. She remembered moving her fingers over the wide-set eyes and full soft lips, the passion that consumed her at the time. I have to get hold of myself.

She reached out and placed a hand on Mike's forehead. He opened his eyes at once and looked straight at Tracy. He took a second to focus, then reached out, and pulled her down on top of himself. She placed her soft lips on his, very much aware of the sensual contact between their close warm bodies. Tracy did not resist, only whispered into Mike's ear, "Please, Mike. We must take a little more time to talk. I'm not concerned about you. It's my own secrets that I fear. I can't have you end up hating me."

Mike removed his hands from Tracy's bottom and helped her stand. "Tracy, I know we have some serious problems to work out. I want you to answer one question first. Are you going to attempt to leave my life again?"

"No, Mike, only if you decide that would be best."

"Would you care to clarify that for me?"

"Not yet. A girl has to keep a few secrets, you know."

"Okay. Give me a few minutes to brush my teeth and tend to business here, and I'll meet you topside. One more thing, Tracy. I believe you knew that I loved you when we kissed goodbye two days before Christmas in 2004. And I still do."

"Yes, I felt that you did. We were both afraid of commitments. I felt that my life was just beginning after I met you."

Mike freshened himself up and joined Joel on the bridge. "How're things in our house of 'what next?' tonight, Joel?"

"So far, things couldn't be better. All systems check out well. I started the water maker for a while. We should run it the rest of the night and tomorrow. I logged our cruise activity since your latest entry. You seem to have a plan for the girls. Do you think they can pull it off without a problem?"

"Yeah, I do. They are both very bright. We should go over everything with them after breakfast tomorrow morning. Anything new on the weather?"

"Not much has changed. It looks like you were right about slowing down to let that stuff ahead of us settle out some. I backed off to only eight knots. It looks like we can get a full three hundred miles under the bottom before we contend with that pressure gradient. The last hundred miles off point Loma might be a bit rough."

Mike turned to see Tracy with a tray of sandwiches. "Beware of beautiful angels bearing gifts, Joel. There may be a broken heart hiding behind that smile."

Chuckling at Mike's serious look, Tracy said, "A broken heart means a tender heart, and it can be repaired, with the help of the right repairman. How's the coffee holding out for the single-cup maker?"

Joel said, "Perhaps you could bring out more of the bold roast, Tracy. That seems to go faster."

Mike said, "Tracy, we're missing about a million dollars somewhere. I think I should pat you down. It looks like something's hidden in your bra."

Tracy laughed. "By the time you finished checking out my bra, big boy, you wouldn't remember what you were looking for." She passed Joel a steaming coffee.

He laughed so hard he spilled coffee down the back of Mike's leg.

"That serves him right, Joel. Thanks. Is it okay to take Mike below to check his injury and change the bandage? It won't take long, just long enough to beat him with a stick first." Tracy located the medical kit and placed several cotton pads next to the bottle of alcohol used for cleaning and disinfecting the wound. She turned to Mike and noticed he was still trying to deal with unwanted sexual stimulation.

"I'm sorry, Tracy. This wouldn't be a problem with anyone but you. I'm feeling too emotional at the moment."

"I understand, Mike. I'm also pleased to hear that. Would you like me to leave?"

"No! Just go ahead and let's get this over with." Mike reached for a pillow and held it close while Tracy pulled his fishing shorts down below his butt.

"Mike! This thing is not closing like it should. It doesn't seem to be infected. Maybe the antibiotic has controlled the infection. You'll have a large scar, no doubt."

"That's good, Tracy. Someday as an old man, I can show it to our grandchildren and brag about how it all happened."

Tracy turned away for a moment, wiped her eyes, with a tissue, washed her hands again, returned to place a lengthy section of gauze, and taped over.

Joel stopped in the salon to finish off a thick ham and cheese sandwich before retiring. "Did you tell Mike about the tally that you and Stephanie arrived at last evening?"

"No, I want Mike to ask about it. What's wrong with this guy?"

"You know him, Tracy. That's not what's on his mind since you arrived. He's never been so gentle with anyone. I'm glad to see the interest for both of you."

CHAPTER 14

Afghanistan

2012

The US military reentered Afghanistan in 2008 as stage 3 of America's longest war in history. In 2012 Major Mike McGowin was recalled to his old Army intelligence unit.

The exploding rocket took out the sentry hut at the south entrance, followed by automatic weapons fire. Colonel Findley rolled to his feet at once.

Depending largely on the Afghan military for their primary protection, he was concerned. "What's the situation, Lieutenant?"

"The east wall has been blown out, and they're attacking from two directions. Looks bad, sir. They're using RPGs to breach the compound."

"Hot damn, we don't have enough of our team here for protection. Give me a rifle team. I'll head for the breach in the wall."

Major McGowin, Staff Sergeant Sid Goddard, and their interpreter, Ahab (named Ahab because of his metal alloy leg) were camped about a mile from the village. They assisted the villagers throughout the night, trying to prevent a small reservoir dam from collapsing from heavy rains that flooded over the dam near a concrete spillway—the small lake, a primary source of water for the mountain community during the dry season. Using heavy stone, sandbags, and a great deal of manual labor, soft earthen sections near the overflowing spillway were reinforced.

"Let's go home, Sergeant. I could use about a gallon of coffee and a bucket of bacon and eggs. With the rain gone and the sun coming up, I believe these folks will be able to finish the job without us."

"They should continue with rock reinforcements all the way around, Major. Otherwise, the next heavy rain may just spread the problem out further. I'll have Ahab keep track of their progress."

"That works for me, Sid. Call in Ahab, and let's make tracks."

They approached the Humvee. Sergeant Goddard rushed down to answer the radio that was going crazy with loud yelling from Andy Fagan at headquarters.

"Get Major McGowin at once, Sergeant. This is an emergency!"

"He's right here, Lieutenant. Hold on."

"Major, we were hit hard about two hours ago. About twenty well-armed insurgents blew right past the Afghan army security force and attacked us here at the headquarters building. Colonel Findley led a counterattack against the east perimeter and was taken prisoner after a fierce RPG attack. He was injured. A group of five or six attackers broke away, dragged the colonel with them while the main body remained here, and exchanged fire another forty minutes. The accuracy of our men took a high toll on the enemy before they withdrew into the mountains. Sergeant Moore and the sniper team left with two interpreters soon after the colonel was taken."

"Lieutenant, I want one man to pack enough rations and extra ammunition for our weapons and meet us at grid point

70134211. Sergeant Goddard, Ahab, and I will relieve him of his load there and hike into the mountains behind the sniper team. A two-day supply should be enough. You're now in charge. Keep the head shed well informed. Let them know that I believe a larger force on the scene might result in the insurgents killing the colonel. No helicopters in the air unless called. Now put me in touch with the sniper team. Oh, one more thing, did Sergeant Moore take both scoped .50-cal. weapons?"

"No, Major. He elected to take one of the new M107 semi-auto weapons. He wanted to travel light and move fast. He did take two M24 scoped 7.62 weapons. The rest of the team is carrying M4 carbines."

"Good! Send the heavy .50-cal weapon with four mags and another scoped-up M24 with nine mags. We'll leave the two M4 carbines we have with us. We're going to have a heavy load going up those mountains. Sergeant Godard, Ahab, and I'll be waiting at grid point 70134211."

Sergeant Moore, five other well-trained riflemen and their two well-armed Afghan interpreters pursued the enemy over the first high mountain ridge, then down into a narrow valley. They stopped and studied both the valley and high mountain trails through their magnified rifle scopes. They observed several trails leading down the mountain and a damaged building about 1,200 meters up near the summit.

Sergeant Dick Moore informed Major McGowin that his team had located the group holding the injured Colonel Findley.

"The group of six insurgents with the colonel is holed up in a small stand of trees about eight hundred meters ahead of us, Major. We have good eyes on them and are attempting to get another hundred meters closer without being seen."

"That's good, Dick. If they make an attempt to move out, can you stop them without getting the Colonel killed? I'm afraid that they're slowing to arrange a transfer of the prisoner."

"That may be the case. We think we've located some kind of old house or other remnants of a defensive position much higher up the mountain. That may be their destination. From our current location, if they attempt to move up the hill, we should be able to take out those holding the colonel and drive the others to cover once they expose themselves."

"That's a desperate measure, Dick, but I believe we have to take it. We can be at your position within the next hour unless we run into something unexpected. If it's at all possible, separate the insurgents from our man and protect him at all cost. Pick the bastards off one at a time and flood the rocks around them with M4 fire once the ball starts."

A little over an hour later, Mike and his team near the sniper team's position heard the first loud explosion, a .50-cal. sniper weapon. It's followed right away by a second shot from the heavy gun.

Mike said, "We may miss the action boys. Let's hurry on over the hill. They may need us."

Sid Goddard answered, "Hell, Major, why don't you drop that extra gear for us and hump it to the top with the 50-cal.? You won't need more than three or four mags until we get there."

"Thanks, Sid. Here, you guys divide this ammo up and catch me over the hill. If you find my carcass along the way, just kick some rocks over it."

~~~

Mike reached the crest of the hill and had a clear view of everything going on. The sniper team had separated into two groups of four, about 250 meters apart. They had good defensive positions, keeping the insurgents pinned down in a clump of rocks. Two dead insurgents and what must be our wounded man were lying on the sloping trail just beyond a small circle of trees. He looked through the rifle scope, saw the enemy's small defensive position on the mountain above, observed a larger force of fourteen or fifteen men cautiously moving down a mountain trail from above.

Mike called Dick Moore. "Bad news, Dick. Look up the mountain. There are about fifteen new participants about to join the fracas. I'll stay here and set up the other fifty while keeping an eye on the colonel and you boys as well. I'm sending Sid Goddard and Ahab down the hill into effective range for their M4s. We'll have your back. The new fighters will try to encircle your position once down the mountain. From here, I can discourage the encirclement. Let's put the big fifty to work, Dick. See if we can finish off the original rat pack."

"There are only three left from that group, Major. They've gone deep. I'd like to grab the colonel now while those three are quiet and before the new boys arrive. I'm afraid he may bleed out if we delay."

"Okay, Dick. Light up the area where they're located so I can see exactly where to place my fire."

"They still have a couple of RPGs, Major. I'm a little worried about having them waste one on the colonel in our rescue attempt, unless we kill all three. Fire in the hole, Major!"

Dick Moore placed four successive heavy rounds into the rocks where he believed the insurgents were holed up. It became obvious to Mike that the enemy gunmen were lying prone in a shallow wash through a low outcropping of rocks. From his high position on the mountain, he looked over the area through his scope and lined up on the man in the center position. Mike held a deep breath, relaxed, squeezed the trigger, and moved to acquire the next man ahead. Fired again. He attempted to find the third man, lined up the big fifty, and lowered the muzzle.

"We have a rabbit running for the weapons. Do you have him?" The other heavy weapon vibrated the hillside.

"Your shot took his arm off, Dick. I can finish it for the poor bastard. He fell next to one of their RPGs. That was an excellent shot, a moving target."

"Thanks for the help, Major. One of us will see about Colonel Findley. He's alive, but in bad shape."

"Hold on. Your team on the right has trouble higher up on their right flank. Our heavy weapons may make a difference." It looked like about six of the dirtbags up there.

Dick asked, "Have you located the rest of the bunch?"

"Yes. I make out a total of six more, three to a group following a trail down in front of you. Can you see them?"

Dick said, "They're without much protection, so we can handle them from here. You and your boys help our guys on the flank. I'm sending a man down for the colonel."

Mike turned his attention back to the high ground where the enemy appeared to be setting up a mortar position. His location still remained unknown to the enemy, well protected by huge boulders. He called Sergeant Sid Goddard and Ahab. "I suggest you two join Dick Moore and his team and prepare for mortar fire or RPGs from the mountainside. Also, Sid, make sure the team retrieves the colonel and renders medical care at the first opportunity."

"Roger that, Major, will provide help. We have eyes on them."

"I'm sure you left all of our 50-cal. ammo with me, so once you join up with Dick, find out how he's faring on heavy stuff. I plan to open up on that mortar crew pretty soon and may not have adequate ammo to get the job done. Tell everyone to make careful accurate shots when possible. Good luck down there."

The six insurgents confronting Sergeant Moore and his men must have believed themselves to be outside the range of small arms fire. A series of four shots were fired from extreme range. Scoped M24 sniper rifles in the hands of well-trained marksmen take their toll fast. Three of the enemy dropped to the ground, dead or injured, before the sound could be heard. The remaining three turned back up the mountain, hoped to get out of range, away from the sharpshooters.

Moments later and within a total time frame of seven seconds, loud explosions from the heavy 50-cal. semi-automatic sniper rifle echoed across the valley. The remaining three enemy combatants went down, leaving a small dust cloud rising above where they fell.

From his concealed position, Mike joined in with slow deliberate shots into the suspected mortar crew at a distance beyond his comfortable range for accuracy. He adjusted the scope a little after each of the first two rounds and took out three of the others in five shots. He sent the enemy into a panic, not knowing where the heavy missiles were coming from. Mike continued acquiring targets, creating havoc in the rocks where the enemy sought sanctuary from the projectiles and rock fragments. After five long minutes without another target, he placed one round every minute into the rock formation for the next five minutes. Five rounds fired. Three remaining survivors raced in panic back across the mountain slope.

Mike recognized his own limited skill on the heavy weapon and called Sergeant Moore. "Dick, I let three get away. They are making tracks on the mountain trail and headed back up. Are any of you free to take a few shots?"

"We can give it a try, Major. They're now almost beyond the M24 range. I want to conserve the big .50 ammo in case we have another attack."

<hr />

Without waiting longer, Mike picked up his gear and headed down the mountain to join the others and check Colonel Findley's condition.

The colonel was sedated with morphine and weak from loss of blood, but awake.

"Hello, Colonel. You look like you've been dragged through the rocks and then used for target practice. You mind if I take a look at that hip?" Kneeling next to the colonel, Mike could see that the bone in the man's leg had been shattered just below the pelvic socket with a small-caliber through-and-through.

"Hell, Mike, I felt sure those turkeys were going to put a bullet in my head and leave me for the buzzards. The early-on pain was so intense I thought I was finished anyhow."

"Yeah, Max. I hate to tell you this, but you do have a serious through-and-through. That may mean the end of your Army reserve career, but I believe you will still be an effective special agent with the FBI."

"You think it's that bad!"

"Something to be grateful for. It could have been a lot worse. You can thank Sergeant Moore for the quick pursuit and two quick accurate shots that separated you from the insurgents. I'm going to give you another shot of morphine, and then we're going home the hard way." With three miles of rough terrain down the mountain to the nearest safe evacuation point, Mike and the team agreed to share in turns the awkward weight of the sleeping senior officer between the larger, stronger men. One man at a time would have to bear the heavy burden.

Major McGowin, being the largest man present, volunteered to make the first attempt to descend the mountain slope with their injured comrade.

Ahab commented, "Sometimes being crippled pays off. We have your back, Major."

———

An hour into the hike down, Mike ached from the heavy load and needed a break when Ahab, tail-end Charlie, rushed in to report they were being followed. "Major, the enemy's hanging back just beyond the ridgeline we just crossed over."

Mike ordered his men to spread out and take up defensive positions as he continued down the mountain with his burden. Believed to be well out of RPG range, he stumbled along fast until all hell broke loose. He felt a stab in the back at a point just below the injured man he carried. Neither man wore body armor at this point, having given it up as being too hot and heavy.

Without stopping, he glanced to his left and realized one lone combatant had managed to slip around his men and fire a weapon. He saw a tall turban-clad man holding an empty rocket launcher. In the same instant, the man's head exploded into a cloud of blood and brain matter.

Mike continued down the mountain with his burden. Feeling weak, tired, and thirsty, he saw a shady outcropping of rock. He eased himself down, pressed the injured man against the large boulder behind him, still strapped to his own back. Mike rested in the shade of the rocks, realized this might be all the rest he'd have until his injured friend could be lifted from his back.

After a brief rest, he struggled to his feet, eased himself out of the shadow of the rocks, and looked all around with caution before continuing down the mountain. He glanced at his compass often and prayed for accurate calculations.

Another long hour of torture, he saw a dry riverbed in the distance. Not sure he could make that last four hundred meters, he forced his tired mind to dwell on his comrades in the mountains and prayed that they all arrive safe and soon.

Thirsty and exhausted, he found a single rock in a small clearing where he hoped to be seen by his own people before the enemy could find them. He knew once he left his feet, he wouldn't be able to rise again. His last memory—a call for helicopter evacuation. The pain, excruciating, he kneeled and passed out.

CHAPTER 15

Agent Findley

June 18–19, 2015

Mike used the satellite telephone aboard *Blue Dolphin* to call the personal number of his friend in Washington, knowing the phone wouldn't identify him in advance. He grinned to himself in spite of the seriousness of the call and punched in the numbers. After five or six long rings, he was certain a machine wouldn't be taking the call and grinned again.

"This had better be good, whoever the hell you are!" said the strong, somewhat-groggy voice.

"Drop your cock and grab your socks, Max. I know it's late and the dream's hot, but this can't wait. Don't badger me about disrupting your beauty sleep."

"Damn you, McGowin. If I'd known it was you, I would've turned off the damn phone. Are you under arrest for pissing in public? Just pay the fine, serve the ten days. I'm going back to sleep."

Mike laughed again. "In all seriousness, Max, this is important. I wouldn't be calling you at this time otherwise. I can't discuss the matter in detail over the air. It's important enough to ask that you fly out to California right now and meet with me in confidence. I'm calling from a private vessel in Mexican waters, and I'll be checking in with customs on the morning of the 19th in San Diego."

"That's ridiculous, Mike. You're talking about this morning. It's already 3:00 AM here. I don't believe that you'd waste my time, but I need some help here. Give me what you can in a safe manner so I can make a decision. It may not be possible to get there so fast."

"All I can tell you now, onboard with me are potential witnesses to serious crimes, maybe multiple killings. It could be big, Max. Their lives are in danger, and they can't leave this vessel in safety. You'll not be disappointed in the results of this meeting. I'm sure you have access to an agency jet. Its use will be justified if you meet me at customs and come aboard to interview the witnesses. You may decide how to proceed from that point."

"All right, let me see what can be done in this short time frame. Give me the number of that satellite phone. It's available twenty-four seven?"

"Yes, for sure. Thanks, friend. I look forward to seeing you in a few hours." Mike massaged his temples with his thumbs for a few seconds before reaching for the logbook. Max is a detail man. I have to provide all pertinent information and make it concise. He's not always sweetness and light. Mike poured himself another cup of black coffee and thought more about Max's position now, Deputy Director. He thought back to their last deployment together. A damn fine leader, suffered terribly.

Mike turned off all lighting, including instrumentation, left only radar for light on the bridge. He relaxed in the comfortable command chair, looked out at the smooth moonlit ocean, and let his mind review the situation ahead. An hour later, he walked outside, let the fresh sea breeze stimulate his energy level, and returned to the controls. He felt more certain of a favorable outcome to their problem.

CHAPTER 16

Lance Makes His Move

June 20–25

Augustine Palmyra and Mark Wynn landed at a small airport near Todos Santos, Mexico, for lunch and refueling of the Piper Seneca. Augustine called Lance at once and reported in as ordered.

"Lance, we just finished cruising over the Los Coronado Islands, and like everywhere else we've been, there's nothing at all resembling your big boat—any place in the vicinity of the Coronado's or the mainland. Yes, we've checked all the harbors on both sides of the Baha Peninsula. I'll bet money those damn guys crossed into the US and continued north toward Canada. The caper must've started right after that first meeting with shipping agents on June 16th."

"Okay, August. We have to forget about them for the time being. Come in as fast as you can get here. We're running behind in prepping the shipment. I need you here to make it happen."

"I can be in San Quentin by four this afternoon. Soon enough?"

"Yeah, and tell Mark Wynn to be ready for more work when we get this shipment outa here. Find out if he can get clearance into the US. We're not finished with the Guerrero situation."

Captain Attilio Mendez and Lance Howell sat in the pilot house of the captain's seventy-foot trawler moored at one of the private docks controlled by Lance.

"You understand, Captain, all four trawlers are to be loaded and ready by six tomorrow evening. As usual, each trawler must carry two panga boats on deck, ready but empty of cargo in case any snoopers are checking you out from the air. The entire load of product must be held below until you rendezvous with the freighter. You also have thirteen paying passengers to be delivered ashore between San Diego and Point Conception. It's up to you to determine how they are assigned space in the panga boats with the product. Pass this on to the operators."

"I understand, Lance. Me and Augustine always figure out those things while product's being loaded onboard the mother ship. So you and Augustine will make the trip aboard my vessel?"

"Yes. I'm sure you're aware of my missing yacht and the effort we're making to track down the Guerreros!"

"I know those two, Lance. Somehow this doesn't seem like their kind of planning. Someone else must be a part of it. Have you considered all your key people here and in the states?"

"I've looked at all our people. None are missing, and none seem capable of pulling it off on such short notice. How about some of those trawler owners we've worked with in the past? Do you have any ideas about that?"

"No, I can't think of anyone that crazy, Lance. Are you boarding tomorrow evening?"

"Yes. August may check in with you tonight. I'll be here until the product is packaged and loaded tomorrow. I have the usual meeting with the ship owner's agent at the rendez-vous point. Can you accommodate everyone with margaritas here in your pilot house?"

"Sure. I look forward to finding out what those shippers know, if anything, about that last meeting with the brothers who stole your boat. I know most of those guys."

—~~⌒~—

Augustine Palmira entered Lance's office and waited for Lance to hang up the phone. "I have one bit of good news, Lance. The private investigator we hired to locate the bastard who attacked you in Cabo just called in with his report. He believes the son of a bitch was from a private yacht passing through Cabo, heading back to California. You want this information now or after this delivery's taken care of?"

"I don't joke about this, August. Give me what you have!"

"The detective is Pedro Medina, and he's located a taxi driver that picked up two men near the restaurant where you were attacked. He delivered them to a small restaurant across town. Followed up from there, the two fit your description of the attackers and came ashore from a private yacht moored at the Baha Hotel Marina overnight. The boat departed for California before daylight the morning after the attack. The big yacht is owned by the McGowin Trust in Los Angeles, whatever that is. Do you want him to go on to Los Angeles and locate the specific individuals?"

"Do you have confidence in this information, or is it a shot in the dark?"

"I would say it's as good as you're going to get, Lance, but is it worth the expense? After all, locating your own yacht at least offers the possibility of some return on your investment."

"Fuck the investment, August. This is personal. Have Pedro go ahead and follow up now. I want that information in my hands by the time we return from the rendezvous."

Lance Howell, Augustine Palmyra, and Attilio Mendez stood together in the big warehouse and checked over the large drug shipment being prepared for loading onto the trawlers. Lance answered his phone and moved away for greater privacy.

He returned to the others after several minutes on the phone. "Some serious shit must be happening. That was the cartel's big honcho. All shipments and activity in our operating areas are to be stopped at once. Contacts with Mexican law enforcement advised that American drug people are snooping around inside this part of Mexico. We have to stand down until our people locate the problem and take care of it. The mother ship operation is halted until further notice."

He turned to Augustine. "We may be closed down for weeks. I want you to lock up this place tight. Put extra security around the compound, twenty-four seven. I don't like the coincidence of this and our missing boat. Have either of you picked up anything at all? Those guys may have taken the money, gone north, and sold out."

August said, "Lance, I doubt that. They're afraid of any American law enforcement. They could be hiding out here in Mexico, where they have a lot of family."

"I hope you're right, August. They'd be charged with murder in a New York minute." Lance was hesitant about sharing information with associates. Too much of his personal funds hidden aboard the yacht.

"Get that guy, Mark Wynn, on the phone and see if he can get clearance into California. I'm going to my place in Long Beach to figure things out. As soon as Pedro gets what we need, you come on up. We have a lot to do while waiting for our people to figure out what's happening down here.

Our primary objective now has to be getting answers. We can do that just as well from Long Beach, and I can concentrate on getting to that bastard that attacked me in Cabo."

———～～———

At Lance's fifth-floor condominium overlooking Long Beach Harbor, Lance and Augustine met with Pedro Medina, their investigator. "Yes, Mr. Howell, the man's name is Mike McGowin. He's a member of the McGowin family, a wealthy well-known family in the Los Angeles business community. He's very active in the family corporation with offices on Santa Monica Boulevard in West Los Angeles."

Augustine said, "You may have this tiger by the tail, Lance, but something tells me it's time to turn it loose. Even if he's your man, this thing has an enormous downside. This tiger may have sharp teeth."

"You don't get it, Augustine. The bastard humiliated me in my own hometown. No one has ever done that and lived. Your job now is to find three of the biggest and meanest bastards in our organization to be with me when we confront this asshole. This is too big for big Jake to handle alone. Of course, we'll choose the time and the place."

Lance looked at Pedro Medina. "Pedro, can you find this man and tail him for me?"

"Oh yes. He's away on his boat. His father has a favorite place at Catalina Island. I'll locate the boat. He'll be there. How soon do you need this?"

"I want the information now. If he's there on the boat, that fits in perfect with my plans. You get this fact confirmed and in my hands by tomorrow afternoon, you'll earn a nice bonus. You have a description and the name of the boat, I presume?"

"Yes, sir, I'll do a sightseeing tour by air and locate his boat that way. If we find it fast, I can get put on the ground to make sure he's onboard. It'll be faster if I call you with this information. Is that all right?"

At four in the morning, Lance was awakened. His nearby cell phone rang until answered. Half asleep, he sounded irritated, "Yes? Oh! I'm sorry, boss. It's been a short night." For the next twenty minutes, his only comment was, "Yes, I understand. Yes, I'll handle the problem."

Lance Howell met with Augustine Palmira at a small waterfront restaurant in Long Beach Harbor. "Plans have changed, August. You have to return to San Quentin now and get product ready. We have a new schedule coming tomorrow. They're blaming me for the delay, and it's all because of those two women in Cabo. The family filed a missing-person report and sent agents into Mexico to investigate their disappearance. They were asking questions around Cabo and seemed to know that the girls had been seen in that restaurant. My only choice now is to stay here and finish off the bastards that identified the women from family photographs. Pedro Medina's report placed the big yacht at Twin Harbors, Catalina Island. If the men you have coming are good, this problem should be over within twenty-four hours, then I can get back to more productive work."

Within minutes, three men from Lance's Southern California distributions network arrived for the meeting. "You men understand just what we have to do and can handle it, right? The $5,000 I'm paying each of you may seem like easy money, but let me tell you, this man and his partner won't go down easy. I want him beat near to death but still alive when he sees me put the knife to his throat and push it into his brain stem."

He looked at Big Jake. "We made arrangements with a local fisherman to carry the four of us to the area his boat is moored and plan to anchor close by. The local will use his rubber dinghy to move around, looking the situation over until midnight. Then he'll return with a full report of everything that's happening onboard. After that, it's our problem to solve. We'll use the rubber dinghy to move around until we feel the time is right to go aboard and make things happen. There's no reason for those two men to expect trouble in that peaceful harbor."

Big Jake Hayward, at six feet six inches tall and weighing in with three hundred pounds of undiluted meanness, smirked and spoke to his longtime boss. "Hell, Lance, I think you should call off this extra help here and let me do the job just like we've always done. We've taken care of much bigger problems without any trouble."

"Oh hell no, Big Jake. This is personal, and I want it finished tonight. You may as well know that I'm in trouble with the top people in Mexico because this bastard stuck his big nose into my business. I can't have that happen. I want his ass now."

He looked hard at Big Jake. "You're the best man for the job, Jake, but you're also known as an associate of mine with an outstanding warrant and long arrest record, so don't get picked up. You shouldn't even be here. Can see why this is important to me. I want this thing finished now. You have plenty of backup, so use it. I can't afford a screw up."

Soon after midnight, Captain Shorty Munoz returned with his report. "Two men sat in the cockpit drinking beer until around eleven before going down. They turned the lights out in two separate rooms in the aft section of the yacht. There was nothing at all happening for the hour following lights out. One man was large and muscular, and the other was medium height and slim."

The three big men stepped into the small rubber dinghy and started up the outboard motor.

CHAPTER 17

Mike Plans Ahead

June 18–19, 2015

Tracy raised her head to see what caught her eye and pointed. A young seagull hovered overhead, looking for a morsel of food.

Mike was more fascinated with the breeze playing tricks with Tracy's hair. He resisted a desire to lean over and nibble her ear. "I'm glad we have time to talk," he said. "You know we still have a lot to deal with before any of us feel comfortable with this situation. First, we must deal with the authorities in San Diego."

"I know, Mike. I'm sorry for all the trouble. You've been wonderful to Stephanie and me."

"You and Stephanie won't be safe until everything's handled the right way. Before we get into how much money's involved here, how we've got to handle everything, we have a responsibility to those poor women who met up with this guy, Lance. If we handle that part of the situation, maybe the money part will work itself out. Have you thought about what would happen if anyone tried to deposit large sums of money like we're dealing with into a personal bank account?"

"I've thought about all of this, Mike, but I felt all along you'd work it out. God knows, Stephanie and I could use a windfall, but we'll be all right without all that money. She's not destitute, neither am I."

"So look, the primary consideration has to be for those women whose purses we found. Well, we have to be sure they're still missing. Here's the dilemma. First, we need to lie to the customs authorities in San Diego. I wish there could be another way."

He thought hard for a moment. "You and Stephanie gotta get your stories straight, back up our log entry about meeting you outside the restaurant where you had the bad experience with Lance. After your fight in the ladies' room, you ran outside where you caught us on our way out. That's where you agreed to come with Joel and me back to the yacht moored at the Hotel Baha Marina in Cabo San Lucas. You two had your purses. That's going to be the most difficult part for you. Finding yours along with all the others would be too much of a coincidence. Remember, we had a short cab ride, a couple of miles, to the marina. Nothing about being held on Lance's boat. That'll come out later."

Mike removed his cap and ruffled his hair back. "The rest of your story should be just the way it happened. You should go over the entire story, get you both to tell the same thing. Go over it with Stephanie, so it all sounds natural."

Mike pulled on his beer. "That's not going to be all. You may have to provide the real story to the FBI later. The real story at customs would get us arrested, then months of investigations, possibly involving Mexico. I don't want you thinking about that now. I plan on getting the FBI involved after we're through customs in San Diego, with the real story. Do you feel you and Stephanie can handle your end of all this?"

"Of course we can, Mike. I'm glad we'll get the real story out later though. Do you think the FBI will be able to get Lance Howell?"

"I'm pretty sure, Tracy. We've got hard evidence as well as your and Stephanie's testimony."

Tracy left the deck chair, leaned over Mike, kissed him, sat on his knee, and stayed there. He felt a closeness and sensed her desire to belong. Mike pulled her close on his lap and felt her breath against his hair. They remained there awhile.

Mike relieved Joel on the bridge. Each placed a series of business-related telephone calls to the LA office and work sites. Each man utilized a full hour on the phone, followed by a half hour of serious discussion.

Tracy poured two cups of coffee and handed one to Mike. "Would you like a sandwich with the coffee?"

"Thanks, the coffee's fine for now. Do you feel like telling me how much money we have to deal with from those two bags?"

"I thought you'd never ask. The one and only written list, the one you wanted, we tucked away with your things in the top drawer near your bed. The grand total is an unimagined $1,750,000 between the two bags. Now tell me the truth, what can we expect? Will we be able to share in all that money?"

"I can't promise anything, except if they release some of it, that should go to you, Stephanie and Joel."

"Oh, Mike, I can't believe it. I've never ever expected to have more than a barely comfortable living."

"Remember, no guarantees at this point, but we'll see how it plays out. Listen to me, Tracy. That money won't be as important to you now. You've had a terrible time of it. You could be dead right now, so you deserve what you end up with. Now! Would you mind telling me what's been going on in your life, your personal life?"

CHAPTER 18

Tracy's Secret

June 2015

"Mike, I want you to know, I've kept a terrible secret from you. I've waited, even prayed for this chance to ask your forgiveness. I claim my own cowardice and the desire to not interfere with your goals, your plans with the Army, the career you talked about, for not answering you after we said goodbye."

He looked into her eyes with obvious interest.

She tried to still her nervous hands and took both his hands in hers. "Mike, you have a beautiful ten-year-old blonde, blue-eyed daughter bearing the name of a father she's never known. Please forgive me."

Tracy heard Mike catch his breath.

He dropped her hands, reached for her shoulders, and stared at Tracy. "What the hell's going on here, Tracy? Are you sure about what you're saying?"

"Forgive me, please, I've deprived you of the most cherished blessing life can give us." *She felt her heart pound. Please, God, let him understand.* "Yes, Mike. I named her Catherine. Catherine McGowin. She's your daughter, Mike. I always planned to share this beautiful, lovable, and very bright daughter of ours but couldn't find the courage to face you. I moved to California to live, to hopefully run into you some day."

"Damn you, Tracy. How in hell could you do something like this? We cared for each other!" He turned away. "Or did you hate me so much?"

She tried not to cry, but her tears betrayed her. *Would he understand? Please, God, let him understand.* "I convinced myself that you'd moved on with your life, most likely with a loving wife and children. I dreaded you'd hate me, for not sharing our wonderful child after my terrible deception. My dream of us together, recapturing what we both felt after that short time we had together, would never happen."

Mike continued to stare at her and took in every word. *What is he thinking?* She watched him step to the helm, look at the radar, and gaze out at the dark sea. He came back to her.

"Tell me about her, Tracy. When was she born? Why would you do such a thing? We loved each other. What does she look like? Show me something, a picture. Anything to ease my mind. That's not like you, the girl I knew, fell in love with."

"I have a picture in my purse, Mike. You'll see for yourself."

"Why didn't you tell me all this? I had a right to know."

"Catherine longs to know her father. I can't wait till you and Catherine meet. You will love each other so much it makes my heart ache."

Tracy returned. "Look, Mike. The dimple, know anyone with a little family trait like that?"

He smiled for the first time. "My mother, Tracy. She looks just like my mother when she was young. Even as an adult, beautiful."

"You, Mike! Your own little dimple on your left cheek. You know it, don't you?"

"She asks about her father?"

"All the time, Mike, full of questions. Knows as much about you as I do. She sees you through my eyes."

"It must have been hard for you, all alone, losing your scholarship. I only wish you'd shared with me. That's what love's all about. Sharing everything. I thought I knew you, respected your integrity."

"Mike, if you forgive me, can't we start over, a happy family together?"

"I don't know, Tracy. I feel betrayed."

CHAPTER 19

Tracy's Trauma

2004–2005

Tracy Conwell finished basketball practice for the week and hurried through a shower. She sang out, "I'm twenty-one. Tracy, you're twenty-one years old, get your tail home." She looked at the leggy brunet in the mirror, ran her hands over the flat stomach, and stood there for several moments.

———⌇⌇———

"Hi, Mom, what's for dinner? I'm starved."

"Sweetheart! It's your birthday, the big one. Your dad's taking us to a show at Caesar's, a dinner show."

"Wow, that's great, but can't I get a bite of something to keep my sugar level from dropping?"

"Sure, check the fridge. Oh, got a message for you. Some guy named Mike called to wish you a happy birthday, wouldn't leave a number. He said it was an overseas call, and he couldn't be reached. So who's this Mike? I hope it's someone good for you. You haven't shown much interest in men friends lately."

"Too busy, Mom, I'll get dressed. Gotta tart up for our big dinner."

Tracy sat and stared at her reflection in the mirror. *Glad I wasn't here when he called, can't weaken now. He can't receive calls over there, makes it easier to resist temptation.*

She brushed her long dark hair again. *I have to stay strong, get over this need to be with him. This sickness. Stop crying myself to sleep at night.* She moved to the closet and pulled out her favorite blouse. Someday it'll be different. On my terms, equals.

Tracy said, "I'm surprised we didn't have to wait longer for a booth. Caesar's restaurants are usually more crowded. Can you believe it? I can drink now, even go to the clubs."

Stephanie said, "Can I have your fake ID now? All I have to do is dye my hair."

She saw Mom look at Dad. He laughed. "Sweetheart, you're twenty-one now, old enough to drink, but we don't want to hear about fake IDs or such." He looked at Stephanie and winked. "You, young lady better be extra careful. Using a fake ID can get you in serious trouble. It's best not to go down that road."

Mom said, "Stephanie, please don't think about growing up too fast. You have plenty to do without going to clubs at your age."

"So, Tracy, tell us about this new man in your life."

She looked at Dad, mouth open. "Why would you think there's a man in my life?"

"Your mom and I have seen a change in you. We've talked about it and hope it's for the best. We don't know."

"You're both too sharp for me. I didn't plan on saying anything yet. Maybe it's best while we're all together." She looked at Steph. "Don't talk to any of our friends about this, Stephanie."

Tracy took a deep breath, looked at her family, and pushed her wine glass away. "I met the most perfect man on my visit with Cathy at the U of A. Please try not to judge me, all of you. I fell in love with him even though we may never see each other again. I knew he felt the same way about me. A hopeless cause is just that—a hopeless cause."

"Honey, what's so terrible that you both can't work out any problems?"

"No, Mom, our lives went in opposite directions, already in motion when we met."

Dad said, "Go ahead, Tracy, we're all ears."

"I don't want to tell you his name yet, but it's not a secret, and I'm not ashamed of him. His degree's in architecture, and he's serving in the Army, an officer. I hear from him a lot, but I don't call him. I allowed things to die on their own."

Mom reached for her hand. "But why! Why do this to yourself, sweetie, if you care so much?"

"Mom, you and Dad may not understand. I don't even understand myself. Call it misguided self-respect or my fierce independence. We started out as perfect strangers at a cocktail party and never left each other's side for three days and three nights—the most wonderful time of my life. We knew beforehand that the challenges of life already worked against us. I've thought about this a great deal. Fate allowed our lives to intersect for a moment, those three days. The path of his future pointed away from mine, as if he was being pulled by some irresistible force, and I didn't have the courage to intervene."

"Oh, honey, you're so hard on yourself."

"Mom, Dad, you're the most wonderful parents in the world, so I'm going to need your help more than ever." Tracy took a big swallow of wine. "I visited Dr. Schuman today, and he confirmed what I suspected. I'm pregnant with a child by a man I may never see again. And believe it or not, I'm happy."

Dad got up and left the table. Mom reached across for Tracy's hand as if she were a small child.

Dad returned to the table. "So, Tracy, you don't want to marry the child's father."

"I love him a lot, Dad, but please, both of you, let me make this decision on my own."

Dad sat down. "Honey, you should allow the father a chance to know he has a child coming. He'll be interested if he's the man you think he is. You've got to be fair to him."

Tracy saw the pain in her mother's eyes and watched her Dad take out his big white handkerchief and wipe his face.

"Dad, I'll have to give back my scholarship and find a job. I want to try to finish my junior year before the baby comes. With help from you, Mom and Dad, I fully intend to finish all the required courses in biology and try for a teaching certificate, even if it takes me an extra year."

Dad placed his big hands on her shoulders. "You know you'll have our support, honey. We'll welcome a new life into our home."

Mom dried her eyes with the corner of her napkin. "Sweetie, you have our help as long as you need. This is your future, and we want to be a part of it."

Next day, Tracy called for appointments with her coach, athletic department, and the dean of admissions. Everything went well, though her coach looked pretty upset until she told him about the baby. She talked with Dr. Schuman as a family friend. "Give me a few days, Tracy. The medical community is always looking for bright young people. I'll make a few calls."

A few days later, Tracy interviewed with Medi-Serv Associates, who hired her part-time for the front office in the local surgical center. Tracy continued her exercise regimen without slowing down and worked part-time. She confessed to her friend Brenda: "I'm enjoying the part-time job, but I'm also looking forward to the long hot summer without the stress of school. Mom thinks I need to slow down."

Mom said, "Tracy! Running three miles a day while six months pregnant can't be good for you or the baby. Check with Dr. Schuman and give yourself a break. I'm worried about you."

"Oh, Mom, she's so beautiful!" Tracy said. She held her young daughter for the first time.

"Well, she certainly is. She looks just like you, except the blond hair and baby blues. Catherine is the second beautiful blond in our family now."

"You know she does look like Steph, Mom, when she was younger. Look at that little dimple. Her dad has that. I know he'd feel so proud." Tracy broke into tears, a real flooding.

Mom reached for her hand, bent, and kissed her forehead. "Mom, I pray that I've made the right decision, that the three of us will get together. I know it's up to me to make it happen. I believe he is strong enough to forgive me."

CHAPTER 20

Tracy and Catherine

April 1, 2015

The heat in the Mojave Desert was brutal. Tracy had to stop because Catherine needed lunch; both had to feel hungry. She stopped in the desert town of Baker, where the world's tallest thermometer registered 109 degrees. *Thank God for the Mad Greek restaurant, an oasis for tired travelers*, she thought.

"I need a break from the drive, honey. Besides it's lunchtime, so don't say you're not hungry. I heard your tummy growl."

"Maybe a little."

"Mom, will it be this hot at Gramma's house? I can't wait to get in the pool. Wish we didn't get so hungry so we would get there sooner."

"You know it's always hot at Gramma's house. Put your flip-flops on before getting out of the car, sweetie, won't burn your feet. All your friends will be there to celebrate your birthday."

———

Gramma Mickey said, "It's time for you and your friends to get out of the pool for a while. Ice cream and birthday cake's all ready for you under the umbrella. Come on out before the ice cream melts."

Eight screaming kids rushed past the patio where Tracy relaxed with Stephanie, their friends, Mom, and Dad.

"So, Trace, then you do like living in Los Angeles?" Stephanie said.

"Takes some adjusting. The traffic's bad, but not much worse than here in Las Vegas. The rush lasts a lot longer."

"Was it hard to find a decent apartment in a nice area?"

"We've been fortunate so far. A friend at school put us in touch with the owner of a nice condo in Tarzana. We love it. It's gated, has a great pool, and the owner is nice. Also, Steph, we don't have so many of those days where the temperature gets over a hundred and stays there."

"Sounds really great. How far are you from the beach?"

"About ten miles from Malibu, but I've found a favorite beach area a little farther north. Paradise Cove. Cat loves it there. We try to make it for a few hours every weekend. It's still in Malibu, but a little less congested."

Stephanie took a pull on her pink lemonade. "My friend Valerie teaches at Santa Barbara City College. She's invited me to visit during our Thanksgiving break. Wants a partner for some beach volleyball and hopes I might fall in love with the area as she did."

Mom laughed. "You know darn well that you'll love Santa Barbara. That's where you became addicted to volleyball in the first place. That week we spent at the small beachside motel cost us a small fortune."

"My social life drags right now, and I need a break. Look forward to seeing Valerie."

Tracy raised her glass. "Steph, you make great lemonade." She really has no idea of a boring social life.

Mom said, "I know you and Valerie both played volleyball in school, and I sense that was the beginning of your real dedication to the game. But why do I think there may be more to this visit than you're expressing?"

"Oh, Mom, you're right. I may investigate teaching in the public schools there in Santa Barbara. I only avoided mentioning it because you miss Tracy and Catherine so much. Forgive me."

"Of course, it's time for you to spread your wings and test yourself anyway. Your father and I don't expect either of you to miss out on life's opportunities just because we love you."

Tracy said, "That's wonderful, Steph. Santa Barbara is only a couple of hours' drive for us. We'd love that. Cat'll be thrilled."

"Don't mention it yet, Tracy. I need a job first. That might not be so easy in Santa Barbara."

After all the kids left, Catherine sipped ice-cold lemonade and talked with Gramma Mickey. She changed the subject.

"Mom said my daddy lives in Los Angeles, Gramma. Do you know him? His name is Mike McGowin, like my name. She said we would look for him in LA."

Mickey looked at Tracy, then back at Catherine. "I've never met your father, honey, but I understand he's a very nice man. I'm sure he'll find you soon, with your mom's help."

Oh my god, don't bring that up right now.

"Do you think he'll like me, Grandma?"

"Oh yes, he'll fall in love with you the first time he sees you, honey. If he knew where you lived, he'd come, see you all the time."

"I'm sorry, honey," Tracy said. "I'm sure we'll find him before long."

CHAPTER 21

Storm at Night

June 18, 2015

Blue Dolphin rose high on a large swell and dropped into the deep trough. Mike studied the horizon. Strong winds blew the tops of waves, didn't look good. Bad weather on into San Diego. Damn weather system should have moved on by now. He drank coffee from a thermos cup and studied the wind direction again, a slight change, more from the west, rough. Been blessed with great sea conditions over the last three hundred miles.

Tracy got off the couch, staggered her way to Mike, and gripped his arm.

"Better get ready for more rough conditions ahead, honey. I want you and Stephie to take two Dramamine tablets now, grab a barf bag, and work your way down to your cabin. Less motion down there, and I won't have to worry about you both getting hurt. Snuggle up in bed and try to doze off, but keep the bags handy."

"Seems like a strange storm, only wind and white caps."

"This's a dry storm, sweetheart. We're dealing with counterclockwise winds from a low pressure trough off the California coast, merging with clockwise winds generated by a high stationed over Mexico, known as a pressure gradient. We have to pass through the area between the two systems where the winds hit the greatest velocity."

Mike looked at Tracy and covered her hand with his. "We're going to be very busy on the bridge through this thing, honey. I'll worry a lot less knowing you and Stephanie are safe in your bunks. We could enter a worse mess by midnight."

"Hey, Joel, we bought ourselves several hundred miles of good weather, but it looks like we're entering the area of disturbance now. Please see that our ladies get tucked away in bed, then check the tenders and water toys. Go through the entire vessel, including all galley supplies. Lock all refrigerator and freezers. Oh hell, make sure you double-check everything before joining me back on the bridge. We have a lot to deal with tonight."

"I'm ahead of you, Mike. We expected this, so I started checking things out early. The bilge pumps and fuel filter pressure are good. The engine room can handle anything thrown our way."

"Great, Joel, we're ahead of the game, won't be fighting a heavy downpour. Winds will gust over fifty miles per hour with seas running eight to twelve feet with short intervals." He looked at Tracy. "I'm concerned about the girls."

Tracy turned back to Mike, looking reluctant to leave. "Joel asked Stephie and me to go through the boat with him earlier, Mike. We stowed small stuff in drawers and cabinets, got all the towels and deck chairs off the sundeck, checked the doors and lockers."

"Thank you, girls. Now let's try to ride this thing out without anyone getting hurt."

Stephanie spoke up. "How long do you expect this thing to last?"

"Look, we may have to fight this all through the night, maybe on into San Diego. To be on the safe side, you guys should go ahead and take the anti-nausea tablets, and hunker down until we're out of this mess. Just keep those bags handy. Joel, while you're down below, double-check the scuba tank storage rack. Wouldn't be happy if one of those things fell off the rack, busted the neck off, and shot away like a rocket. Two thousand pounds of compressed air behind it could create a problem."

A strong gust of wind howled through the superstructure above. Wind speed increased. Not even a barbed-wire fence to slow the velocity off the wide Pacific, he thought. High waves and deep troughs will stress the ship and crew. *Blue Dolphin* encountered more pitch and roll. Mike altered course, turned stern quarter to the violence, ran with the sea, and smoothed out the ride. He decided to run that way for thirty minutes, then changed course again, with a west by north heading for thirty minutes. He followed a zigzag course, allowed more stability, moved his eyes from compass to radar and back again, with growing concern for a small target showing up from time to time at three miles, about ten degrees off port.

Mike locked down the helm long enough to fine-tune the radar and got a better picture. Wouldn't like smacking into one of those big steel containers lost from a ship. They lose them in bad weather sometime. *Where's Joel? he should be back by now. Must have a problem down below.* He adjusted course, checked radar again, unknown object now at quarter mile, he changed course once more placed object in water down wind on starboard side. He picked up high-resolution glasses.

Joel grabbed the helmsman's chair. "Sorry, Mike. The steel cage door protecting the scuba tanks banged open, a broken latch. Had to round up some repair gear and reposition the tanks, came close to a disaster. The girls are using the bags. I left some extra with dry towels and a damp cloth for each."

"Good man. It looks like we have a vessel in distress out there. Look for a weak light blinking off starboard. I'll take the glasses up front for a better look."

Saltwater blanked the windows in front. Mike turned on the freshwater wash and allowed the wipers to do a better job. The situation became clear at once. "I'll be damned, Joel. Someone's signaling with a weak flashlight. Slow to minimum headway. Let's figure this thing out. No doubt his radio's down. I got nothing all night on channel 16. That looks like a thirty or forty-foot sloop with the mast dragging in the water, people in the cockpit."

"Hope they're all wearing life vests, Mike."

CHAPTER 22

Pick Up Survivors

June 19, 2015

With his binoculars, Mike studied the storm-ravaged vessel. "That damn thing's on the verge of sinking. Don't waste time, Joel. The sea's too rough for a vessel-to-vessel rescue. The trough's too deep, the frequency too short. Here's what we do, only way to do it. Take control, Joel, now. Keep her downwind of the other boat, our swim platform about twenty-five feet away from the debris hanging over the side."

"I can manage that, pal. I'll have to use the cockpit controls. What do we do next?"

"I'll pass a long line over to the people in the boat, our end secured here. If I yell out loud, you know the line's in the water, too close to the propellers. Move us forward as slow as you can until I've recovered the slack. Then get in position again for another throw. We don't have a monkey fist. That would make it too simple."

"Mike, that boat's filling with water, sinking. Go with the line over now."

With safety harness in place, Mike held a coiled one-hundred-foot ski tow rope, hoped the handle was heavy enough to make the thirty-foot toss, yelled at Joel.

"Get on the hailer. Have them tie one person at a time to the line, loop it through the space at the handle, pull it tight under the arms of the first person to go. I'll pull them over and up."

Joel turned on bright lights in the superstructure, lit up the entire area. Mike made his first throw. A tall guy grabbed the line and looped it around the nearest woman.

Mike yanked the woman over the side into the water. She flailed about, terrified. He took up slack at once and pulled her toward his platform. His safety harness allowed him to put his full strength into the pull. The woman came in close. He let out a small amount of slack and allowed the rolling wave behind to dump her at his feet in a foot of swirling water. He released the line and guided her into the cockpit.

Mike recoiled the line, making a second toss to the other boat. The same man made an accurate grab. The waterlogged vessel rose on a large wave, tore the line from his hands, and threw him into the boiling sea between the two boats.

Joel pulled *Blue Dolphin* farther away when the stricken sailboat rolled down the trough toward the man in the water. Joel's voice blared, "She's filling with water, Mike. Everyone needs to grab the next toss."

Mike recoiled the line and tossed it to the two people in the sinking boat. One in the water motioned for the others. They grabbed the line and jumped in his direction, struggling to hold on. Mike saw the trio grab each other's life jacket with one hand, holding the line tight with the other.

Blue Dolphin rose high on a swell, threatened to come down on top of people in the water. Mike let out slack as she slid down the trough, then pulled all three people onto the swim platform in a foam-covered mass. They looked blue, chilled, moved slow, with hyperthermia.

Safe aboard, the survivors watched their stricken vessel disappear beneath the waves. Joel saw they were in the cockpit, eased the *Dolphin* away, turned into the wind, and reduced the roll.

"Good job, Joel," Mike said and helped the shivering refugees into the salon. He was pleased to see Tracy and Stephanie standing there with large dry towels. "We've got to get these folks below and outa the wet clothes. Get warm blankets. Wrap them up well, and we'll meet you in the salon with hot coffee."

George Hampton explained that he and his wife, Susan, were unfortunate owners of *Southwind*, a fine forty-one-foot sloop. He introduced their fellow survivors, Frank and Doris, their cruise guests for the past month. Then expressed his gratitude for responding to their needs in such professional manner. "We lost hope, then the lights of your vessel appeared."

"George, you're aware I have to report the abandonment and sinking of your vessel. Do you have any objections?" Mike said.

"No, of course not. Our families will be pleased to hear that we're safe aboard your yacht. Thank you again, Mike."

Mike asked Tracy to take charge of the group and excused himself to join Joel on the bridge. "I have to call in this incident to the coast guard in San Diego. You did a hell of a job at the controls, Joel. No one could've done as well. If I can't raise the coast guard by sat phone this time of night, I'll go to the emergency radio frequency."

"This is US Coast Guard, San Diego California. How may I help you, sir?"

"Coast Guard, this is the US-registered yacht *Blue Dolphin*. Owner, the McGowin Trust of Los Angeles, California. I wish to report a rescue at sea of four persons from a foundering vessel. Can you take the report?"

"Yes, sir, Captain. What is your name, please?"

"My name is Mike McGowin, one of the registered owners of this vessel. If you would allow me please to provide you with the information I have, then I'll attempt to answer all further questions. There's no longer a danger or further risk to life. We have taken onboard, the following persons—Mr. and Mrs. George Hampton of Pacific Palisades, California, and Mr. and Mrs. Frank Morris of Santa Monica, California. I found no obvious injuries that need immediate attention. The vessel was abandoned at longitude 31 minutes, 59 seconds north and latitude 117 minutes, 34 seconds west. Heading from San Diego is 180 degrees, due south, approximately 65 nautical miles from San Diego and 50 miles west of El Pescadero, Mexico, on a heading of 256 degrees west. We're now underway for San Diego and anticipate arriving Coast Guard there not earlier than 5:15 AM or later than 6:30 AM, Pacific time. Yes, in answer to your question, you may reach us at the number given any time between now and our arrival time. Thank you, sir. This is the vessel *Blue Dolphin*. International documentation number confirmed. This call complete."

"Mike, you go down and take care of things below. I can handle it here. We'll run with the swell a short time to reduce roll."

"Okay, Joel, I'll get fresh coffee to you right away. The stabilizers are helping now that we have good headway, running with the wind."

Stephanie saw Mike on the stairs. "How's Joel?"

"He's tired and stressed, Stephie. Can't get away from the helm long enough to get coffee. Could you make it up topside with some of those sweet rolls? Use the single-cup coffee maker in the upper salon for his coffee. Hold on tight, okay? We don't want an injury after everything else you've been through."

Mike reached for the coffee and sweet roll offered by Tracy and sat down near George and Lucy Hampton. "I'm sorry for your loss, George. Gotta be tough losing such a fine vessel."

"Yes, like losing one of the family. Lucy and I've pampered her for twenty-seven years and enjoyed every minute of it. Of course we're grateful that our friends here, Doris and Frank, survived without serious injury."

"Do you mind telling me about it, George? I'm curious how such a fine vessel can flounder."

"Well, we entered the storm area over twelve hours before losing the mast. The wind grew too strong to keep sufficient sail for adequate headway, so we engaged the auxiliary power, used a little sail as a steadying factor. We seemed to be weathering well. Around ten at night or shortly thereafter, what I believe to be a huge rogue wave caught us broadside with those strong winds. We rolled far enough into the trough to dip the mast. It held us there, flooded the cockpit, threw seawater down into the cabin. That's when we lost the radio." George coughed hard before speaking again.

"Within a minute, she tried to right herself. The mast snapped, followed by a cracking and scraping noise. It caused me to think we may be losing the keel or the hull breaking up. The engine continued to run for a few minutes, then died. We had lights in the cabin for a bit longer after that, tried to figure out what to do next. No one panicked, Mike. I could not feel more proud. Aleck, Dana, and Lucy stood steadfast throughout the entire ordeal."

Mike listened to the story. "By the way, George, I'll enter your account of the disaster into our ship's log. That'll remain a permanent record should you require as much for your insurance company. I expect you'll have a long tiring session with the Coast Guard in San Diego. Let me know if I can be of any help to you."

Mike thought of his own problems to deal with in San Diego. He counted on his old buddy Max getting there to help work out a solution.

CHAPTER 23

FBI Gets Involved

June 19, 2015

Assistant FBI director, Max Findley, presented his credentials to the agent behind the desk, Port of San Diego. Mike wouldn't bring me out here for a damn boondoggle. This might be interesting.

"Captain McGowin and his vessel participated in a rescue at sea during the early morning hours, Agent Findley. Would your appointment have anything to do with that rescue?"

Not sure, Max hesitated. "I believe our business to be a separate matter. Captain McGowin has a relationship with the bureau office in Washington. I can wait until his vessel is cleared, if you say so."

"We're familiar with the captain and his vessel. Help yourself to coffee and whatever's left in the lounge. Shouldn't be long, sir."

Max watched agents come and go from a large plate glass window and wondered what's going on.

The door cracked open. "Captain McGowin has cleared customs, Agent Findley. You may board the vessel."

"Hi, Max, you look like Harvey the six-foot rabbit with those red eyes."

"Don't push your luck, Mr. Yachtsman. I could arrest you and bill you for my expenses. You better have a damn good story."

Mike introduced Joel, Tracy, and Stephanie. "Give us a moment to ourselves, guys." He took Max to the pilot house for privacy. He moved to the overhead console, checked all the ship's communication systems, and made sure none of their conversation could be overheard.

"So this is how the privileged live, how elegant!" he said, giving Mike a hearty embrace.

"Hell, Max, I chose my old man carefully, so I could enjoy the good life. Good wine, bad women. Better fasten your seat belt, Max. I'm about to tell you a strange, almost unbelievable story. I'll give you everything and rely on your judgment."

Max expected this to be solid, or he wouldn't be here. "Let me get my recorder set up, Mike."

"The two women you just met were kidnapped and held on a boat off the coast of Mexico. Joel and I became involved, aided their escape from members of the Mexican drug cartel holding them. We have evidence of more missing American women who have either been sold into the sex trade or murdered."

"I hope you can back up all this, sounds hot. Was that sailboat crew involved?"

"No, Max. The large plastic trash bag there on the deck holds water-soaked handbags, complete with identification for nine individual American citizens."

"Hold up a bit. Let me see what you have, Mike." He pulled out one of the women's bags and raked through it. "Okay, move on, Mike."

"They're all women, I believe, taken and held the same as Tracy and her sister, Stephanie. The other two canvas bags contain an unbelievable amount of hard US currency, liberated from the Mexican drug cartel that held these women to be sold as sex slaves. I believe the leader and their kidnapper's Lance Howell, an American citizen operating with the Mexican cartels and having strong organizational ties on both sides of the border with Mexico." Mike stopped and drank from a water bottle.

Max said, "I may not arrest you after all. Go on with the story."

"I expect you to understand why I've had to keep this closely held within the confines of this vessel. Both women remain in serious danger, Max. This guy Howell believes Tracy Conwell's dead in accordance with his instructions."

Max held up his hand. "I have to interrupt with a few questions. What instructions?"

"Howell ordered his henchmen to use her anyway they wanted, then sink her body. This is only part of the story, Max. Let me finish. He and his associates are scrambling to figure out what happened to the boat carrying the sisters and the cartel funds. They had the cash for some kind of payoff to shipping associates who moved their cargo-loaded panga boats north. I'm sure you understand why we could not ask assistance from the Mexican authorities."

"Well, Mike, I'll say this for you. It's a hell of a scenario as you describe it. I assume the women can back up everything you say. How involved is the other man?"

"Joel works with me as an associate and personal friend. He's as involved as I am. You'll understand when you get their stories."

Max snapped off the recorder. "I think we can delay the personal interviews for the time being. Okay! Let's talk generalities before the interviews. You may be creating a hell of a lot of work for me, Mike. I may never forgive you."

Mike returned the grin. "You've been a good friend. I thought you'd want to share in some of the fun since you FBI guys lead such boring lives in between the political hoopla around Washington."

"So . . . what do you expect to happen to all that cash you 'liberated,' as you put it?"

"Well, I'm counting on that big brain of yours to help work something out. I'd call it just compensation for the traumatic experience suffered by the sisters, and I'd like to see an equal share for Joel Santiago. He placed his life in jeopardy without question when faced with the consequence of failure to act."

Max paid close attention to the story and made a few quick notes on a small pocket pad. Mike, always responsible, looked after his friends. *Got to bring in DEA soon. This situation could be bigger than I thought.*

"Look, Max, I appreciate your quick response as a friend as well as the ultimate professional. For my part, I want those guys caught, justice for the missing women. The cash has to be secondary. We could have avoided telling you about the windfall, no one would be the wiser. There's no record and no outside knowledge of the money. Only Howell knew of the cash that he'd stashed until we discovered it, searching for evidence of the missing women."

"Let me give some thought to this, Mike. First, of course, I have to interview the other three participants. Then I need to verify a few things through DEA. Looks like you stumbled into something."

"One more thing, Max, you need to know I have to keep the sisters hidden on board the *Blue Dolphin*, continue on to Ventura County with a one-night layover at Catalina Island. *Blue Dolphin* will be more difficult to locate if the cartel is looking for vessels returning to San Diego or Los Angeles ports from the area their asset is missing. We'll delay docking at our home port in Mandalay Bay until we have a good handle on this thing. Would it be possible for you to come with us to Channel Islands Harbor in Ventura County?"

"Hold on a minute. That might be a little much," Max said.

"You'll have full access to the satellite telephone plus cell phone service once we reach Catalina Island."

Max thought for a moment. "I have a rental car here, Mike, and my bag is still at the hotel. Stay here a couple of hours while I sort out a few things."

"I can arrange for a temporary delay through the Harbor Department. Once you're back on board, your interviewing can go ahead as planned."

Max returned with a small travel bag. "You should know the news media back there are making a lot out of your rescue of the crew from the disabled sailing vessel. They're going to blow your cover." He looked around at the two women. "That's for sure if their interview of survivors drops names of your present company. You hold tight a little longer. I'm going back in and talk to those survivors."

"I should've thought about that. Thank you, Max."

Max returned forty-five minutes later. "I spoke with the survivors, and they'll cooperate. I was also able to convince the Coast Guard and customs people as well. All parties have agreed to be cautious in any conversation with the news media or anyone else asking questions."

Mike said, "Let's hope for the best."

"The survivors are discussing their ordeal with a few people in the courtesy lounge, waiting for relatives, Mike. The media people are still getting organized. I don't think it'll develop into a problem."

"Thanks, pal. Let's make a getaway before they start looking in our direction. Glad to have you with us, Max. I'm concerned about the safety of these women."

CHAPTER 24

San Diego North

June 19, 2015

The heavy vessel sliced through the five-foot swell rolling down the gulf of Santa Catalina. "Hey, Joel. Take the helm into Avalon. Radar's tuned down to a quarter mile, shows several small fishing boats around the kelp beds," Mike said. They'd left San Diego bay before the fog cleared. "Max might have more questions for me during the interviews. I'll stay with them through the first go-around."

Mike sat across from Max, who established procedure for interviews with Tracy and Stephanie.

Joel's clear voice came out of the speaker above. "We're increasing speed to twenty knots, Mike. That'll smooth out the ride a bit and make it three and a half hours to Avalon Bay."

"Gotcha, Joel."

"So, Max, let's use the main salon for your interviews. That's the lowest level in the boat. The pod drive systems eliminate vibrations, but the engines make only a low hum."

Mike sat through Tracy's interview, answered a few questions himself. The preliminary questioning went well, so he and Tracy returned to the bridge.

Tracy followed Mike topside and talked to Joel at the helm, yet to be interviewed. She looked over the approach to Avalon Harbor.

"This place is gorgeous! I've never seen anything like it." Avalon Bay looked flat and calm. She pointed at the gauge registering outside air temperature—a pleasant seventy-four degrees. They awaited permission to enter the harbor.

"Joel, why would you ever go to Mexico when this island paradise is only a few hours away?"

"Ya know, Tracy, I often wondered the same thing. Mike's dad started making the voyage to the Sea of Cortez to fish the waters around La Paz and Puerto Vallarta years ago with his fishing buddies."

"Well, thank God you made this trip with Mike for the sake of our daughter," she said.

Mike listened to the easy conversation between Tracy and Joel from his position on the couch behind them. *Why in the world did I ever fail to persevere in my effort to reach out to her years ago?* Because he'd convinced himself she'd found someone else, he never got over the short intense affair.

Joel said, "Avalon Harbor Patrol's moving another vessel from our mooring. It'll be another thirty minutes before we can pick up the wand."

Max came up from below. "Hey, Joel. What's going on up here? Thought something interesting was happening, didn't want to miss anything. I've wrapped up interviews for the time being."

The radio blared, "*Blue Dolphin*! Avalon Harbor Patrol. Your mooring's now available. We'll stand by for assistance should you require any."

"Thank you, Harbor Patrol. We'll move into the harbor now," Joel said.

"Mike, take her in while I grab the wand. I can work the spring line back to the rear tie down alone."

Mike maneuvered the big vessel into the harbor, eased down the narrow fairway, turned into an even more narrow space between the bow of boats on one side and stern of boats on the other side. *Blue Dolphin* spun on its own axis and nosed up to a tall wand sticking up near a floating buoy. He watched Joel reach down with a gloved hand, pull up the wand attached to a heavy looped mooring line, and drop the loop over a stout mooring post. Joel moved to the stern, followed a thin strong spring line to a heavy looped line for the stern cleat.

The radio on the bridge blared again. "*Blue Dolphin*. You appear to be secure. Have a nice stay."

"So, Max, you're good on the interviews for today?"

"For now. Tomorrow, we go over each interview again before transmitting the recordings to Washington with my report. It's so important to check everything for consistency before sending it. I want your candid comments during the review."

"A point of interest to all of you. Checking the identification on each of those women whose handbags you turned in. Families have already reported them missing within the past three years. Furthermore, this man Howell has been under suspicion from drug enforcement for more than five years, which lends even greater credibility to your stories and the evidence regarding those missing women."

Mike said, "Confirms my suspicions, Max, doesn't make me feel so good."

"Now, Mike, do you serve cocktails aboard this fancy hotel?"

"Do we ever! The sun's beneath the yardarm somewhere in the world. I presume interviews are done for the day, Max?"

Tracy jumped up. "Look, over there. Did you see that? The tall guy in the water, near the dock, he stood in the bow of the dinghy. A swell lifted it away, and he stepped right into the water. His fancy captain's hat floated out of reach. Why are all those people laughing?"

Joel laughed. "He was showing off in front of those girls in the little boat. Now his nice yachting outfit's too soggy to visit a nice restaurant."

Max looked toward the beach. "I wonder what the poor people are doing today."

Tracy smiled. "There may be a few less of us for you to worry about, Agent Findley, if you're as bright as Mike thinks." She touched his forearm. "Thanks for your help and understanding of our situation."

"Hey, Mike, let's get the bar going," Tracy said. She helped Mike at the bar, made drinks, and passed cocktails to the sundeck.

"It's great to have a few minutes alone in here with you. How do you like Max?"

"He sure asks a lot of detailed questions. Some I had no answers for. He's very nice, Mike."

"He's like family, Tracy. We can count on his help. Have you been in touch with your folks today . . . and our daughter?"

"You know darn well I call or text every day, if possible. I should have kept you informed."

"We've been busy, too busy to share personal information, fill the gap in our lives. I want every detail about your life, Tracy, all that I've missed, you and Catherine. We have to make time for that soon."

"I know, Mike. I'm anxious to share everything, get to know ourselves together as a family who loves each other. Let's start with a call to Mom and Dad." He looked at her without answering.

"Mom and Dad went crazy during that long period those awful men held us on that boat. Thank God Joel helped us make a call right after we found Steph. They tried to decide what to do. Mike, would it be all right if I tell them about you? Maybe we can both talk to Catherine tomorrow."

"Tracy, just remember you and Stephie are in hiding, and your life may depend on everything remaining that way until the FBI and the other agencies close up the investigation of the kidnapping and all the smuggling organization." Mike needed to explain his concern, needed answers coming from Max's wide range of contacts through DEA.

"Let me suggest this, honey, to begin with. Tell your parents you and I are together, and you'll give them details later. Then let me explain the necessity of secrecy. If all goes well tonight, we can talk to Catherine tomorrow. Go ahead, take the drinks outside, explain that we're making a phone call before leaving for dinner. We'll talk to your parents, then follow up tomorrow."

Tracy made the call to her mom and dad. "Hi, Mom. Yes, everything's good. Stephanie is here. I have someone with me, Mom, so let me talk for a moment. Then I'll put him on. He'd like to talk with you and Dad. It's very important. I'm with Mike McGowin, Mom. Yes, he needs to explain something, and then we'll talk more tomorrow. Yes, Mom, things couldn't be better. Is Dad available to pick up the phone with you? Okay, Mike will speak with you, and we'll talk with you both tomorrow. Here's Mike."

"Hello, Mrs. Conwell! Yes, I'm Catherine's father, and I'm about ten years late with an introduction. May I call you Mickey? Thank you, Mickey. We're with the FBI right now with limited time to explain. Both of your daughters are safe, but I have to stress how important it is they remain in hiding until the FBI can arrest those responsible for what happened. The bad guys may phone you. Tell anyone you think strange or suspicious that both your daughters are in Mexico and express concern that you've not heard from them since June 10th. And stress this point with your husband. That pertains to anyone who may inquire about either of the girls."

Mickey said, "Would you like to talk to your lovely daughter? She's anxious to know you."

"Thank you, Mickey. You can tell Catherine that she has a father who loves her, can't wait to see her and hold her in his arms now that he's found her. You can expect a call sometime tomorrow from all of us. Tracy, Stephanie, and me too."

"I'm so happy, Mike. You must think I'm foolish after hiding both Catherine and me from you all those years."

Stephanie rushed in to Mike and Tracy. "What did Mom and Dad say about Mike? Were they surprised?"

"More than surprised, Steph. Mom was shocked when I insisted she talk with Mike. I know she and Dad will love him. Dad was out, but they're anxious to talk to us tomorrow."

Stephanie turned to Mike. "I hope you like our family. We're all a little nuts most of the time. That's why we need you to keep us out of trouble. I'm so happy for Catherine. Now she has a good daddy to look after her."

Mike woke early, slipped out of his stateroom without disturbing Joel, brushed his teeth, took a quick shower, and entered the galley. He made two full pots of coffee and poured both into a large vacuum-type decanter. Then he selected a variety of sweets from the pastry case and placed everything on a large butler's tray with paper napkins and plastic plates. He carried it all to the sundeck, set out the drop-leaf table in the adjacent salon and went to where Tracy was sleeping.

He kissed her soft lips to wake her without disturbing Stephanie. She opened her eyes, encircled his neck, pulled him close for a moment, and eased out of bed.

Mike looked at all the preparations. "I must be crazy. You know, of course, we're all having a big brunch over the water at the Busy Bee restaurant?"

Tracy slipped into his arms. "Yes, but it isn't even seven o'clock in the morning. The rooster hasn't crowed yet. I think you're just hungry, lover boy, maybe didn't sleep either. I'm so excited, Mike. I can't wait for your conversation with Catherine. Bet she didn't sleep a wink last night."

"First, I didn't sleep either, and second, I'm starved, and third, I want to tell you I love you and I'm overwhelmed by everything."

Grinning, Mike pulled Tracy down on his lap. "I'm still mad at you, so get rid of that happy face." She wrapped her arms around his neck, kissed him furiously. They held each other close.

"I'm glad you got me out early. We can have some time together before anyone else wakes up. I want to stay on your lap while we have our coffee."

"I would love that. He smiled and placed a light kiss on her lips. I'm so happy to have you back in my life, never stopped missing you, never even dreamed we had a beautiful daughter. Now a new beginning."

"I know. I've never been more certain of anything in my life. Catherine will love you the way I do. She's dreamed of her father the way I dreamed because I talked about you and described you almost as you are today. You're not much different from the man I fell in love with, maybe a little bit harder to resist."

CHAPTER 25

Max's Decision

June 22–24

Max connected his phone to the charger and looked around the anchorage before joining the group drinking coffee on the sundeck. He reached for the tray offered by Stephanie, a mug of black coffee, bagel, and cream cheese. "Thanks, Stephanie. Sure looks good." He looked at the others. "We have to change plans for today in light of how fast drug enforcement jumped on the information provided by you lucky ladies. I had a long night on the phone with powers that be. Things are coming together fast now, much faster than expected."

"Mike, you've been identified by Howell and his crowd. They're out for blood. We have to be damn careful now."

"I'm not surprised they found me, Max. In California yet? Any indication Howell found out about Tracy and Stephanie?"

"They appear to be unaware of the sisters, believe the Guerrero brothers hijacked Howell's boat for the cash on board. Smart money says Howell's on his way to property he owns in Long Beach. This guy owns a shit load of property in California. We're trying to identify them all."

"Whoa! Man, that doesn't leave us a hell of a lot-o time to prepare a proper reception."

"Furthermore," Max said, "the cartel's cancelled all deliveries out of Mexico. Put a crimp in DEA's plans."

Mike said, "What the hell brought that on?"

"We don't know where, but any communication between our drug enforcement and Mexican authorities goes straight to the cartels. But we can't operate in Mexico without going through them first." He looked around at Mike. "Of course you knew that already."

"This changes the game, Max. We're responsible for the women now. You know Howell's coming after me."

"So, Mike, you still taking us ashore for breakfast? After that, I want everybody together for a review of your statements. Get that out of the way."

Mike looked up. "Good morning, Joel. How goes it this fine day?"

"Good to go, whaassup?"

"Max has some news. Got a lot going on."

Max washed down a bite of bagel with a large swallow of coffee. "I've got no doubt you're all anxious to know what's to be done with that large sum of money recovered from the cartel."

Tracy said, "Didn't forget Max. We just pushed it aside. Didn't think it would work out for our benefit."

"Well, if you happen to generate a little interest, the FBI agreed to pay a reward for information leading to the disruption of a major drug distribution system funneling drugs into the US."

Max studied the girls and their composure. "Once the investigation is completed, each of you, Tracy, Stephanie, and Joel, will receive a deposit into a special retirement account. The net amount of $406,666 will go into each account. Our negotiations with IRS determined, accepting the funds in this manner would provide you with the greatest benefit. That's the best I could do."

"Come on, say something," Mike said.

Max said, "Now's the time for questions or forever hold your peace, so to speak. A letter from the IRS becomes part of your agreement. Believe me, the IRS share taken might have been much bigger."

Tracy and Stephanie jumped up, reached for Joel, and danced him around and round. They all laughed together and brought Max and Mike into the melee.

Max stepped away. "Now don't go running your mouths off about this or the deal's off, ya hear?"

Stephanie hugged Max and kissed his cheek. "Never expected to have anything but an empty bank account. Thank you, Max."

Mike moved toward Max. "Do you have anything casual in that small bag you brought aboard?"

"Not much, I plan to pick up a few things on shore."

"You'll be okay, but make sure you dump the coat and tie for the time being."

The shore boat roared up to the rear of the big vessel, slowed down at the last minute, and eased against the swim platform. With standing room only, the operator yelled, "Everybody, hold her like you love her. Squeeze in tight now. We have two more pickups."

Mike pulled Tracy in tight. The crowd swayed back and forth with motion of the boat. With a full load, the operator nudged the boat up against the pier and sent the noisy crowd scrambling into the heart of Avalon.

The meal finished, Stephanie moved to the outer railing and fed bright colored fish swimming below. A fat seagull landed on the rail post near her. She and the large bird looked at each other for several moments before the bird reached over, plucked all the bread out of her hand, and flew away.

"Darn that guy. Did you see him? I can't believe the audacity. No wonder he's so big and fat!"

Mike had to laugh. "Stephanie, you know they discourage feeding the seagulls."

"Shut up, Mike! You saw him take it right out of my hand." She laughed. She had the same laugh as Tracy. "Do we have to leave so soon?"

"Afraid so, Steph. We can make a quick stop if anyone needs anything special," Mike said. "Okay then, let's hit the dock, maybe see more of Avalon before we have to get back to the real world. What do you think, Max?"

"We really don't have time to enjoy ourselves now. Maybe after I check in, see how things have developed."

Aboard *Blue Dolphin*, Max made several calls and shared information on what he learned. "Things are developing very fast now. Howell has a private detective from Mexico tracking Mike and Joel. We have men on him but haven't decided what action to take."

Mike looked at the girls. "That puts a whole different light on things. Is Howell's man on the island or the mainland?"

"As of now, he's in Long Beach. Howell has a condo there. Drug enforcement advises caution. They don't want us interfering with their plans. Their plan lets the narco operation start up again, catch the whole group in one big net. Tracy and Stephanie, I want you both in a hotel here under my name. Joel, you'll stay there as well to look after the ladies," Max said.

Joel got up and paced. "Mike . . ."

"Wait. Let me finish before your questions," Max said. He pointed at Mike. "You and I will move *Blue Dolphin* to Isthmus Harbor near the west end of the island to lead Howell and his thugs away from Tracy and Stephanie. Any connection between you ladies and Mike or the *Blue Dolphin* would mean an automatic death sentence for you. Because if he finds out you survived in Mexico, he knows that means his own death sentence. Howell's detective is well qualified and must not locate this boat and report the description of two women Lance would recognize in a heartbeat."

Mike said, "Then we got to go soon. After we move away from Avalon, it'll be safe for you to move about here." He looked at Max. "Better leave a tender for them, don't you think? Moving around's often safer than hiding in one place. Joel has a credit card. They all have cell phones."

He looked at Joel. "You have a company credit card, Joel. Use it for yourself and both of our special ladies. See no reason why we can't stay in close contact."

Tracy grabbed Mike's arm. "Please be careful. I can't have anything happen to you now that we've found each other again."

Max passed a card to Joel. "Our people will let us know if the threat grows, but it's important you memorize the sheriff's phone number. Are you okay with that?"

"Of course, you keep us in the loop, and we'll do the same. How about you two? Will you be all right on the boat?"

Max spoke first. "Mike and I will be fine. You three probably won't need the help, but an undercover agent arrives in Avalon tomorrow morning to watch for trouble here. You won't meet him unless he feels a threat to you. He'll have your phone numbers."

Mike said, "Each of you pack what's needed and get going. We're moving to Two Harbors within forty-five-minutes. The sooner we get away, the safer you'll be here."

CHAPTER 26

Task Force Able

June 22–25, 2015

"Mike, you are under no further obligation to continue in this fiasco. I hope you understand. Your yacht could suffer damage. You could even be injured. You brought me in. You may soon regret it," Max said.

Mike laughed. "Look, Max. This is all too important. You did say DEA found the evidence credible, the idea solid, so let's move ahead. I understand what we're dealing with."

"We're asking you for a strong commitment here. Task Force Able has agents from the FBI, DEA, and a huge network of agents inside Mexico, straight up the west coast, all the way to the Canadian border. You're only part of this operation because of your knowledge of the area and the depth of your recent involvement."

"I get it, Max. I agreed to play the part of a staked goat, draw Howell into the net, but the sisters stay well away from the action."

"All right then. I'm aware of their importance as witnesses and their precarious situation. They'll be kept away from the danger area. If you're in, then quit sweating it, Mike. As your friend, I hate to see you involved with this mess at all."

"You've got to know I've given this a lot of thought. Wouldn't have suggested it otherwise, Max. Go ahead, plant the story through your contacts in Mexico. The credible report of two women, last seen in a brawl at a restaurant in Cabo San Lucas on June 10th with known cartel members. That's a damn good reason for DEA operating in Mexico. We're willing to take our chances."

"DEA agreed that's the direction to go, Mike. We close down the investigation, leak the information back through Mexican authorities, a dead end, see if the drugs start flowing again." Max scratched his head. "I'll needle task force leaders again, get the go-ahead."

"Time to crap or get off the pot, Max. Too late for more brainstorming. Enough debate. Make the call. The more I think about it, the more certain I feel the plan will work. The facts back it up, and the cartel has all of the facts. Surely, TF leaders know that."

"It's crucial that survival of both sisters remains unknown to Howell, for the success of our operation as well as their long-term safety," Max said. "That uncertainty's delayed the decision."

Mike said, "Big trouble's coming. All these guys are bad news, Max. We need to be ready, without the obvious security personnel on board to give away the show."

"What're your thoughts on this guy Howell, Mike?"

"I know he's a coward who loves to play the heavy with women. I also know he's deadly. He'll hit hard with his goons along to make his part easy. He carries a knife and has experience using it. God, he's bad news. A real killer, Max, so don't make the mistake of giving him half a chance. They'll come by dinghy or other small boat between one and four in the morning, want to catch us alone and asleep."

"Okay, Mike, let's give some thought to defending ourselves here on the yacht. Our undercover man watches from midnight to eight in the morning, starting tonight. He'll be riding nearby with a harbor patrol boat and operator. They'll have an unobstructed view from one row back and two rows over. He'll report all activity." Max looked out at the nearby moorings. "My guess is he'll pick up our visitors as soon as they show, if by boat. Our agent on the mainland keeps us well informed, so far. Let's hope he continues."

"Thanks for help with mooring, Max. You've always kept yourself in good shape, so let's shake off some of this tension and take a few laps around the boat." He wondered if the old hip wound gave Max trouble.

"That sounds good to me, old pal. Swimming's been my exercise of choice since that last frigging deployment. You have everything on board. How about an extra swimsuit?"

"You have a choice. The water is pretty cold here near the west end of the island. We'll be okay for a half hour or so. Any longer and I'd suggest a lightweight dive suit. I'll go down and throw out a couple of options."

Mike returned in a Lycra swimsuit cut above the knee. Max hung up the phone and looked at Mike. "How the hell do you hold onto all that muscle tone, Mike? I was impressed eight years ago. Now I'm even more impressed."

"A lifestyle, that's all. I run three miles every Tuesday, Thursday and Saturday. I work out on the heavy bag Monday and Wednesday, then rest up with a one-hour swim at five thirty every morning that I'm home. It's a damn boring lifestyle, but I'm addicted, Max."

"You still teach hand-to-hand combat tactics to the officers in your unit?"

"Yeah, a six-session course offered once a year to reserve officers willing to spend the time at regular meetings. A deadly serious undertaking, not your normal self-defense tactics."

"What about women in your life? You must make time for that. As I recall, it was another one of your addictions."

"I see a few women, one a little more frequently than the others, no one special. I know what I want, just hasn't been there. Starting to look better now. You still seeing that attorney in DC?"

"Nah, life got complicated, and she moved on. I miss her. We aren't going to be hit before tomorrow evening at the earliest. Let's get our swim in, and start the cocktail hour," Max said.

"So you know, Max, the Harbor Patrol boys frown on swimmers in the fairways. They're not going to give us guff if we stay around our own vessel."

Mike descended to the rocky bottom forty feet below, turned his face upward, and rose to the surface with a few slow kicks from long legs.

On the surface, Max said, "Go through your usual routine. That's what I plan to do. Know damn well I can't keep up with you."

Mike nodded, dropped ten feet below the surface, swam the length of the *Blue Dolphin*, and surfaced for a breath of air.

Mike thought about Howell's thugs and what might be expected. *He knows Max will try to limit his exposure to risk. Can't have that limit participation, he'll be needed. Max faces task force bureaucracy, a hindrance to getting the drugs flowing again. Using the Cabo debacle as a reason for agents in Mexico is solid. He believes Max's pressure will get things moving again.*

Max put the phone down. "Howell's detective just left the island. He's been staked out on that hill above the USC research center since eleven this morning, giving us the eyeball with binoculars. Let's hope his report to Lance was favorable."

"There's no way Howell's gonna miss out on this chance at me, Max. We have to be ready."

In Port San Quentin, Mexico, Augustine Palmira struggled to have packaged product ready to meet the next delivery. Not able to reach Lance, he called drug lord Federico Quanta with his problems. They are resolved quickly with new orders.

"Augustine, we've lost confidence in Howell. Can you handle things there without him?"

"That won't be a problem, Mr. Rico. I know all the important contacts on both sides of the border."

"His problems with women have cost the organization time and money. We can't have that. I'll be in the Port San Quentin office by nine tonight. This could be profitable for you. We have a lot to talk about. You need not be concerned with Lance and his problems now. Just tend to our business."

CHAPTER 27

Federal Agents at Work

June 27–30, 2015

Mike kicked back with a cold beer and looked at a bikini-clad blonde handling mooring chores on an arriving sloop, and he picked up binoculars for a better look.

Still pushing buttons on his cell, Max called out, "Lance Howell and three very dangerous associates are headed our way with mayhem in mind."

"Yeah, then shit's gonna hit the fan soon. Tonight, I think. I know you have a plan, Max. Why don't you call the others on board and get us all on the same page?"

"My thinking too. It's time for a last-minute briefing. You need to know the good guys from the bad guys before the action starts."

After introductions, Mike invited everyone into the enclosed salon for privacy reasons. "Hey, guys, the sun's beneath the yardarm. With Max's permission, the bar is open."

Max said, "This first." He leaned against the bar and looked at each man one by one. "In cooperation with the Harbor Patrol, Undercover Agent Haskell, you and the DEA agents ride the harbor patrol boat. Flynn and Palmer, dressed as weekend tourists, you will join Agent Alder on a sport fisher moored on the opposite side of *Blue Dolphin*."

Max hesitated. "All right, listen up, duty requirements regarding alcohol get tabled for the next hour. Duty starts at sundown. An open bar is too damn distracting."

With drink in hand, Max went on, "This bunch is dangerous, so don't get careless. Take them as petty thieves. We have to stop them from entering this vessel at the moment of boarding. We make arrests at that time and not a minute before."

Agent Palmer spoke up, "Are you sure they won't turn and head back to the fishing boat, try to make a run for it? That's about what you'd expect from these dirtbags."

Another agent raised his hand. "Once we identify ourselves, the futility of running should be obvious. Our drawn weapons should trump whatever they have."

"Things don't happen that easy. Lance Howell and Big Jake Hayward smell blood and are coming in with the attacking crew. Both have too much to lose. Either one will kill you or be killed before he gives in to an easy arrest," Max said.

Mike stood. "Gentlemen, this guy Howell's known to use a knife. I expect that to be their choice of weapons, less noisy."

Max continued, "Don't expect an arrest unless one or both guys get serious injuries. We have a hard confrontation ahead tonight. Make sure you wear your vest and any other protective gear that's available. Even if you find yourself in the water, it may help against knife slashes. Are there any non-swimmers present? No? That's a positive. Some of us may find ourselves swimming before this thing's over. Mike, since you're the intended target, I want you up top as far away from Howell's knife as possible, at least to begin with. Agent Haskell, you and your two agents from DEA utilize the heavy RIB to block forward motion of the attacking boat. Nose up to the front as fast as possible. Agent Flynn, you and Agent Palmer utilize the harbor patrol boat to prevent their backing away."

Max said with a wink, "I'll remain on the lower deck. Me, myself, and I, Max, along with my trusty Sig will prevent entry onto the yacht. Remember, when the action begins, have weapons drawn and ready. Most important, stay in constant contact with no sound. Be ready to move once the attackers approach the boarding area of *Blue Dolphin*. I'll key all mics at that point and move in quickly. Until then, we keep a low profile."

The meeting ended. Mike shook hands with each man. "Good luck. It's my pleasure to work with you, gentlemen."

Max grabbed his arm. "Let's you and me have a look around the area from above, where you'll start out. You can observe and report from there."

At sundown, they watched agents Flynn and Palmer begin a slow patrol of the area outside the harbor.

Soon after ten thirty, Max received a report from Agent Palmer.

Mike listened to the report and picked up high-resolution glasses, followed a fishing boat with several large men on board approach the anchorage.

Max advised the Harbor Patrol to avoid creating suspicion, allowing the fishing boat to moor where it could be observed by agents. Within minutes, Mike made the first positive ID.

"Max! That's Big Jake Hayward, spitting image of the wanted poster." Moments later, he saw a rubber dinghy launched and head into the harbor with one person on board. From his high position on the bridge, Mike tracked the man in the small boat and passed everything to Max, who relayed it to the other agents.

Agents Haskell and Carter continued to watch the men in the fishing boat. They made positive ID's on all but Lance Howell.

Max said, "You don't suppose he sent these guys to do his dirty work alone, do you?"

"No way, Max! This is too personal. He wants my blood. I believe he's keeping a low profile for the time being. He'll pop up like a bloated fish carcass soon as the action starts. Let's grab a six-pack of beer and sit in the cockpit, acting like everyone else until that guy feels comfortable."

The lone individual in the rubber dinghy motored around the boats and moored inside the harbor, sometimes gliding past where Mike and Max sat, close enough to nod a hello. At last, after resting at the pier-side dock for thirty minutes, he headed straight back outside the harbor and passed close enough to slide his fingers along the slick side of *Blue Dolphin*.

Mike looked at his dive watch, past midnight. Won't be long now. He donned a thick above-the-knee short-sleeved wetsuit, answered a call from Max, strapped a razor-sharp dive knife to his right calf, and entered the salon.

Max placed the still-active telephone on the bar in speaker mode. "What the hell are you up to, Mike? We don't have time to play games. There are four extra big men headed our way in that little rubber dinghy."

"I'm prepared to end up in the water. And you better get yourself ready, Max. I don't expect action until after they check out everything around us. We'd better stay out of sight for a while longer." Mike watched Max disappear into the salon, the only entrance to the yacht through the open cockpit. He flattened himself on the upper sundeck, had a good view, looked out at the men in the dinghy, and passed it on to Max. From his high position, he watched the rubber dinghy pass alongside *Blue Dolphin*, and he saw the men look around the open decks. They moved on toward where DEA agents were hunkered down, prepared for action, in the sport fisher. The heavy load created a wake large enough to rock the smaller boats nearby.

Mike called again, "They're getting impatient, Max. It could happen anytime now. They're looking at the boarding area. Ready your men. They're headed this way, slowing down, Max. Yes. They're eyeballing the landing area." Then louder, he said, "It's a go, Max. Now, Max, now! Go, go, go!"

CHAPTER 28

The Devil Claims His Due

June 28

Fast-moving agents converged on the men in the rubber boat, but not fast enough to prevent two large men from leaping onto the swim platform with weapons and run through the cockpit toward Max.

In dim light, Max faced the attackers, gun drawn. "Federal Agents, hands in the air."

Agents from both teams pointed weapons at the men in the boat, shouted, "Federal Agents! Hands in the air!"

Demands were ignored. Two men jumped into the RIB with DEA agents, creating instant confusion in the dark. Close vicinity and poor light caused agents to delay firing and endangered their own.

Howell's men took the advantage. They slashed agents in the boat with filet knives, creating more panic.

Mike saw the confusion. He turned a switch, flooded the area with bright light, and saw two men attack Max. "Hands up!" The order was ignored. The big man nearest Max swung a steel pipe and struck Max's hand with the gun. It fired. The blow caused the bullet to miss center mass where intended and shattered the assailant's left collar bone before exiting the back. He fell against the port rail, hurt, not out of the fight.

Mike dropped into the cockpit, saw the blow to Max's gun hand, recognized the second man, saw him move toward Max with a knife held low, blade flat, a throat slash. He shouted, "Hey, woman beater!"

Lance! Mike rushed him, faked a kick, appeared off balance, dodged a swipe with the knife, stepped back, and raked a razor-sharp dive knife of his own across Lance's knife-wielding upper arm. He severed the bicep tendon to the bone and saw the knife drop. Mike looked toward the big man at the rail and saw him go for Max's gun. Mike picked up momentum, rushed the big man lifting the gun, slammed him hard, and carried him over the railing, into the water. Both sank beneath the dark surface.

Mike popped up, looked around, and heard shouting. He saw a violent knife fight in the inflatable. He slipped under the water and came up next to the boat. He saw one of Lance's men holding an agent for protection against gun-shots, slashing at other agents. Mike reached up from the water, slashed the cutting arm of the knife-wielding assas-sin, followed up with an arm-around-the-neck and down-ward pull into the water. He returned to the surface and saw a shot fired from the agent in the bottom of the boat strike the remaining assassin in the temple, sending him over the side. He ignored the injured assassin in the water and looked for Max on board *Blue Dolphin.* He couldn't find him. He rushed to the swim platform, passed Big Jake straining to hold onto the rubber boat drifting free. He entered the main salon and saw Max ward off a weakened still-violent Lance Howell, who'd recovered his knife and attacked again using his left hand. Max held him away with the aid of a long-handled deck brush.

Mike yelled, "Lance! You son of a bitch! Don't know when to tap out, do you?" Lance turned toward Mike and received a powerful blow to the rib cage from Mike's strong left leg. He broke the same three ribs injured in Cabo by a blow from Mike's right leg. Instead of falling to the deck,

Lance fell against a large bait tank and remained standing. He struggled for breath, positioning his knife for another attack.

Mike said, "Drop the knife, Lance." Seeing a move in his direction, he stepped forward with a quick faint to the head and severed Lance's left bicep. Both arms now useless, Lance Howell lowered himself to the bloody deck and stared at Mike McGowin. "I'm not through with you yet, you bastard!" Mike had his doubts about that. He looked around and saw Max pick up the knife.

Two FBI agents assisted the wounded DEA agents and ordered a one-armed survivor to remain where he was, holding a grab line from the RIB.

Max pointed. "Look at that! Big Jake's trying to slip away in the dark."

Mike said, "Don't let anyone shoot me, Max!" He dived into the dark water and remained under. He popped to the surface near a line hanging from the rubber boat. He towed the boat partway back toward Max and the other agents. He realized Big Jake had pulled himself into the boat and was attempting to start the small outboard motor. He released the towline, slashed long cuts in both floatation chambers, one side and then the other, and swam back to where agents were watching. Big Jake was left struggling in the sinking rubber boat.

Mike looked up from the water. "There are medical kits in each stateroom, Max, and another larger one on the bridge."

"We found some, Mike, but I think we'll need more if we hope to save Lance and your other slash victim."

Agent Flynn towed the sinking RIB with Big Jake hanging on. His left arm useless for swimming, he appeared submissive.

Mike bent over the sinking RIB to help agents remove the three-hundred-pound man from the water. He leaned forward and reached for the man's belt. He was grabbed around the neck and was forced down deep into the dark water between the two boats. Agents above watched, unable to assist. A full minute passed. Agents stared at the black water. A long arm reached up and grabbed the aft mooring line. Then a big head appeared. Mike struggled for breath. "I need a little assistance here with this dead weight." He lifted his other hand above the water and held a thick ankle with an enormous foot attached.

The two uninjured agents took charge of the heavy body and maneuvered it onto the swim platform. Max said, "How the hell did you manage that? We thought for sure a recovery effort was going to be needed. I've seen you in the water enough to have some hope, but even I was beginning to have doubts."

"Max, I simply relaxed until he gasped a few times and drifted away. It was pure luck I felt a pants leg on my first effort to reach out. I found it necessary to change hands on the way up. He's so damn heavy. I almost released him before seeing the glow above. He should have taken better care of himself."

Max said, "Agent Haskell and two DEA agents have been hurt, one with serious injuries. Everyone was cared for in the main salon, and we used most of your medical supplies, Mike. One of your victims just died from loss of blood at the triage station, believed to be Lance Howell. His remains, along with other dead, have been moved to the Coast Guard boat."

Max dispatched sheriff's deputies and Harbor Patrol to arrest the fleeing fishing boat captain less than a mile from the Two Harbors anchorage. A US Coast Guard cutter from San Pedro arrived in time to assist in the arrest.

Mike poured fresh coffee for Max. They watched curious boaters gathered outside taking in the bright lights and noise. He knew harbor patrol officers had a story of attempted high-jacking for the gawkers. Mike listened as Max arranged a flight to Washington.

"You've made some new friends very happy, old friend. Relax and finish your coffee while I prepare to get us underway," Mike said.

"This thing isn't over old pal o' mine until the fat lady sings. I have a lot of work ahead. Thanks to you."

"I'm sure you do," Mike said. "Documentation and justification's gonna choke a horse."

In Port San Quentin, Augustine Palmira talked with Federico Quanta for the third time in one day. "Push the delivery up one day earlier than planned, Augustine. The threat is no longer there. No human cargo this time. Load every bit of product available. It's needed across the border now."

CHAPTER 29

Avalon, Catalina Island

June 30, 2015

Tracy shifted position, facing away from the morning sun. "So we agree to play tourist today. Let Joel share his local knowledge and drive us around in one of those little open-air jeep-style vehicles. Right, Joel?" The small open-air restaurant overlooking Avalon Harbor was crowded with boaters.

"You two have another cup o' coffee while I make a deal for one of those things that isn't worn out. They're very popular, and the newer ones go first."

"Don't rush, Joel. We may have a Bloody Mary while waiting. It's so pleasant sitting here, looking at the boats and watching all the people. We'll work on our tan some more."

Stephanie said, "Tracy, I feel so darn grateful. You, Mike, and Joel all came after me. I'd given up after you disappeared. The last few days, we've been part of one miracle after another. Neither of us ever put a great deal of emphasis on our Christian religion, did we?"

Tracy shook her head. "I'm like you about that, took it for granted. With all the near misses and amazing things happening, I'm convinced it was more than just luck. Maybe there is a greater deity. Mike came back into my life, both our lives spared, the unexpected financial security that may come with it. It's a second chance at life, sis, for both of us. I know people wouldn't believe what we've been through. It was really hard on Mom and Dad." Tracy thought about the new beginning with Mike. She hoped she could make things work and was worried about the danger facing him now.

Joel parked, walked to where the girls were, and paid the tab. "We don't have a lot of time, girls, but you have to see the view from the Wrigley Mansion first. If time allows, we can visit the Zane Grey house next, then the gardens near the old-time Chicago Cubs practice field before visiting some of the more interesting shops."

Tracy said, "What's the rush? Don't we have all day?"

"We do, but the glass-bottom boat ride and the trip inland to the buffalo herd will take up the afternoon. It's going to be a busy day."

Tracy woke early. She had trouble sleeping. She couldn't stop thinking about the danger Mike was in. She showered fast, avoided waking Steph, and went downstairs for coffee. Dressed in white shorts and halter, she turned heads sitting alone at a table near the busy sidewalk and answered her cell.

"I just had a call from Mike," Joel said. "They're fine. He wouldn't share much information, said they had a lot to tell us."

"Thank you, Joel. Do you mind if Steph and I hang here this morning? We would like to try those buffalo burgers you were bragging about for lunch. If that's okay with you, we'll meet you at Erick's on the pier."

Erick's Café on the pier proved to be crowded with people. Some leaned against the railing, drinking beer, looking down at colorful fish in the clear water and the few sun worshipers on the small beach below. Joel, Tracy, and Stephanie sat at a small table and watched the hustle and bustle of tenders loaded with people move between vessels in the crowded harbor. They munched buffalo burgers and drank cold Mexican beer, unaware of the mayhem the night before at the other end of the island.

Joel picked up his phone, the second call of the morning from Mike. "They are only a few minutes away from the harbor." He ordered four buffalo burgers to go and looked at his companions. "Max had better be quick, or Mike will eat all four of these things. You've seen him eat, haven't you?"

Tracy jumped to her feet. "Oh yeah! You should see him in a steak house. Joel, do you mind if we rush on down and wait for you in the tender? I'm anxious for all the details they wouldn't share with us over the phone. One of them could be injured, and we wouldn't even know."

Joel caught up with Tracy and Stephanie. "Tracy, you're as nervous as a long-tailed cat in a room full of rockers. You aren't happy to see that big guy, are you?"

She laughed. "I've struck gold, Joel, and it's not the bank account either. I made a huge mistake hurting Mike as well as myself the first time around. Can't lose him again regardless of anything else that might happen."

The bright sun reflected around the shiny vessel as she came to a stop in the outer harbor. Max hugged each of the women with one arm.

Stephanie said, "I've never seen a prettier picture. You guys should have seen *Blue Dolphin* approaching into the bright sunlight out of the mist."

Stephanie climbed out first and noticed the bandaged hand. "Max! What in the world is wrong with your hand? Let me hold the tender."

"Okay, Stephanie. Hold tight to the rail while I give Tracy a hand up."

Delaying entrance into the harbor, Mike waited for Tracy and Stephanie on the bridge. He kissed Stephanie on the cheek, lifted Tracy all the way off her feet, and placed a firm kiss on her lips.

Stephanie pummeled Max. "You've had trouble. Tell us what's going on."

Mike said, "Hold on, there are lots to tell. Let us get on the mooring first."

Joel tied the tender alongside and rushed to join the others. He delivered a brown bag and a six-pack of cold beer to the salon, where they waited for information.

"Hey, guys, there's buffalo burgers in the bag."

Tracy jumped to her feet. "Sit down, you need a little pampering." She gathered potato chips from a food storage locker, plastic plates, and napkins for each. She placed two buffalo burgers and a beer on a tray. He delivered one to each weary-looking man and looked at Mike's unshaven face. "Look at Mike, Steph. He looks almost as scary as the big unshaven man that hoisted me off that patch of seaweed in Mexico." Eyes tearing, she kissed him on the cheek and sat down close to him.

Max related in graphic detail everything that happened. With full knowledge of the terrible ordeal inflicted upon Tracy and Stephanie at the hands of Lance Howell, he explained how the man's life finally came to a just end. "He bled out on board a small boat carrying him to a triage station set up on the pier at Two Harbors."

Stephanie shivered, attempting to relate how she was taken in by that smooth-talking attractive man she first met at a beach volleyball tournament in Santa Barbara.

Tracy said, "Max, what do you plan to do now? I hope you'll be able to stay around a few days."

"There's too much unfinished business, Tracy. I've arranged to be picked up at 5:00 PM from the old seaplane terminal. Coast Guard has provided a helicopter ride to LAX for an evening flight into Dulles International near Washington, DC. We have to finish this job while everything's in motion."

After a quick shower and shave, Max returned to his friends, tired but ready to travel, again dressed with the discarded coat and tie.

Tracy was the first to give him a big hug. "Max, I feel like we're all family here. By now, I'm sure you're aware that Mike's the father of my beautiful daughter, Catherine. I haven't been asked, but I am going to marry him. Can I count on you at our wedding?"

"I'd never miss your wedding, Tracy. If he gives you any trouble, let me know, and I'll have him arrested, so you and I can get married instead. Remember, a little snow on the roof doesn't mean there's not a fire in the furnace."

Mike spun Tracy around, dropped to one knee, and placed both hands together beneath his chin. "Tracy, I'm crazy in love with you. Will you marry me?"

Tracy stepped back and looked down at Mike. "I don't know. Are you sure, Mike? I do have another offer waiting, you know." She grinned at Max, pushed Mike down onto the deck, and sat on his stomach. "I accept, but I also want sworn statements from all the witnesses here."

Stephanie said, "Let him up, Tracy. You need to help me with the cocktails. We have to celebrate with a toast before Max's shore boat arrives."

Max congratulated Tracy and Mike on their wise decision. Stephanie poured five brimming-full glasses of white wine for the toast.

Mike talked with Max while waiting for the water taxi. "I believe my part of this thing is over. You will keep me in the loop, won't you? For the finish. And thanks, Max, for all you've done here."

Max wrapped his arms around his friend. "No, thank you for bringing this thing to us, old buddy. I knew I could count on you for a little excitement. Somehow, Mike, your troubles always involve beautiful women."

CHAPTER 30

The New Family

July 1–2, 2015

Mike saw the SUV drive into the guest parking at Marina Del Rey Yacht Club. He gulped down the last of his coffee and moved for a better view. He looked a second time at the pretty little girl who rushed past a tall man to look around. It had to be Catherine. "Tracy! Come up now, I think they're here."

Stephanie and Tracy hurried past Mike into the open arms of Harold and Mickey Conwell.

Mike overheard Catherine. "Does my daddy live here?"

"No, sweetheart. This is a yacht club where people keep their big boats," Mickey said. "Your father has a guest slip here for today and tomorrow so we can all get to know each other." Catherine ran to her mom.

Mike dropped down on one knee down to be at eye level with Catherine. She appeared shy at first, then rushed into his arms. "I'm so sorry, honey. It's taken a long time, hasn't it?" Catherine was shy but curious. She sounded like a grown-up talking. Mike continued to carry her in his arms like a tiny tot, both afraid to be separated. A beautiful child, strong family resemblance. He spent time with Catherine before turning back to introduce himself to Mr. and Mrs. Conwell. He hugged Mickey with one arm, used his left hand to greet Hal, and continued holding Catherine until she's called by Tracy. He gave her a tinder kiss. "Go on with Mom

185

and Gramma, honey. We will always be close now. I'll see you again in a few minutes."

Mike and Hal relaxed in the salon alone. Hal expressed his gratitude again and asked for more details surrounding Tracy and Stephanie's stressful period of captivity and rescue. Mike shared information and felt a comfortable familiarity with Hal. He admired his warm sincerity.

Tracy hugged her mom again. "Aren't you glad to be aboard with us now?"

"It's very nice, honey. We weren't sure about being away for more than one night. She laughed. That was some heavy lobbying by you and Mike that brought this about. Hal and I have never been aboard any boat overnight."

Mike looked at his watch. "Cocktail hour must commence soon. We have one short hour before our dinner reservations at the warehouse."

Stephanie and Tracy rushed to their bar duties. Tracy suggested red or white wine from the cooler.

Mike said, "How about a good Scotch, Hal?"

"It's about time, and a martini for Mickey. She isn't called Martini Mickey without good reason. And, Mike, I like any man that appreciates good Scotch."

Mickey accepted a dry martini and raised her glass. "Thank you, Mike, for looking after our girls."

Hal placed a hand on Mike's shoulder. "You have my grateful appreciation as well."

Mike looked at Hal and Mickey. "I love, Tracy, very much. Is it all right with you if we get married right away?"

Hal looked at Tracy. "You love him?"

"Of course I do! Remember what I said to you and Mom so long ago?"

Hal raised his glass. "I regret it's taken so long, Mike. Welcome to our family. You've made Tracy very happy."

Tracy approached her parents with tears in her eyes. "You both have always been there for me. Without you, Catherine and I could not have held out. Now we also have Mike, who loves us. Thank you, Mom and Dad, for making it all possible. I really do believe in miracles now."

Mike picked up Catherine and placed a soft kiss on the tip of her nose. "Your mom and I are getting married real soon, so that we can be a real family like I've always wanted."

"Will we all live together like Gramma and Poppa?"

"Yes, sweetheart. You, Mom, and I will always be together now. Is that okay with you?"

"I can't wait for my friends to meet you. Is it okay, Dad?"

"It sure is, honey. I want to show you off to my friends too. You'll soon get to meet your cousins, who'll love you. And you'll also be meeting Grandpa Marcus, my dad. He can't wait to meet you! When school starts, can I go with you the first day?"

"Sure, Dad, I hope you will, and maybe Mom too."

Dinner at the Warehouse, Mike ordered champagne, poured for toasts, and insisted Catherine be seated between himself and Tracy.

Tracy said, "Mike has been in touch with his family. He's worked out a family gathering. It will be a casual, relaxed setting."

"My father reserved time at the Pacific Corinthian Yacht Club in Channel Islands Harbor. Tracy and I felt it was important to have everyone get together as soon as possible. Dad will be thrilled with Tracy and Catherine. Mom would have loved them."

Joel eased *Blue Dolphin* against the one-hundred-foot concrete dock at the McGowin home in Mandalay Bay. The corner lot, with most taken up by the three-story main house and guest house, left only a thirty-foot strip of green lawn between the sea wall and rear parking area. A drive-through beneath the guest house accommodated parking for four cars on a concrete apron in the rear.

The quiet approach of *Blue Dolphin* caught Barbara Blair and Marcus McGowin unaware. Barbara was surprised by voices coming from people lining the yacht's railing. She and Marcus were having coffee on an eastside nook near the kitchen. Barbara alerted Marcus, and they rushed to greet the new arrivals.

Mike led Catherine up the ramp toward his father, with Tracy at his side. The others followed down the stairway and up the ramp to the flagstone walk leading into a shaded patio where everyone gathered. Barbara Blair approached Catherine, smiled, with hand extended.

"Hi, Catherine. I'm Barbara, and this is your other grand-father, Marcus. He'd like for you to call him Papa or Papa Marcus, but first, he wants a great big hug."

Mike introduced Tracy. "And this is Tracy, the mother of our daughter, Catherine, and our many future children. Dad, she's forever the love of my life, so please don't smother her with that beard. I'd like to keep her around for a while."

Tracy moved toward the huge bearded man now holding Catherine on his hip. Before she could grasp his hand, a long arm encircled her shoulders and pulled her tight against a solid body.

"You two have made me the happiest, luckiest man in the world. Tracy, I intend to love you both so much it may make your mother and father jealous."

Hal said, "I'm already feeling the pain, Marcus. These two have been such an important part of our lives. I'm Tracy's father. This is my wife, Mickey. And it looks like we've gained a son! We've already adopted Mike into our family."

Marcus released Catherine and Tracy to embrace Hal and Mickey. "Welcome to our family, Hal. My home and heart will always be open to you and Mickey."

Stephanie nudged Hal. "Marcus, this is our other daughter, Stephanie. You already know the full story. We'll always be grateful to Mike and Joel, who rescued our daughters. We're proud of their courage and tenacity through the ordeal."

Marcus said, "It's well justified. They confronted the devil and rendered justice the old-fashioned way."

"The loss of our two daughters would've been tragic. We would never recover from such a loss," Hal said.

Barbara took charge and moved everyone into the wide-open family room with a view of the harbor. An excellent hostess, she had refreshments ready with chilled white wine and cold beer.

"Please, everyone, relax here with Marcus a while before I show you into the guest house. You'll be able to rest and freshen up before dinner."

Phil and Sally Robinson arrived with their children, Samantha and Brett. With them were Bob and Gayle Alder and their daughters, Sara and Tanya.

Barbara made the rounds, pointed out just how fast the afternoon had flown away. "It's time to get ready for the party! Hal, will you and your beautiful ladies follow me out to the guest house? You can get yourselves settled in."

The Crow's Nest at the Yacht Club and shaded portion of the outside deck were reserved for the McGowins' party.

"Hal, let's see what Dad has ordered up in the way of good wine."

Marcus said, "All you beer drinkers may wish to try these favorites of mine. I have a 2009 Dark Star Anderson Road that's been breathing for about an hour, or try the Hunt Cellars 2002 Syrah. Both are excellent. You may decide to give up beer all together."

With all glasses filled, Marcus said, "Drink to the Conwell family. May the bonding be permanent, the future bountiful, dreams attainable, and life's short journey filled with joy."

Harold Conwell said, "To the McGowins and their warm welcome. Thank you, Marcus!"

Mike's cell phone vibrated, he went out to get away from the music. "Yes, this is Mike McGowin."

"Mr. McGowin, this is Bruce Briggs with your home security service. At nine forty-five this evening, we received a signal here alerting us to a breach of the alarm system on the west patio doors of your Calabasas home. We alerted the local police and sent our nearest roving patrolman to have a look. Soon after, we received a call from the Calabasas police officer arriving on scene. He reported that our security patrolman had been ambushed and killed just outside the damaged entrance to your house. The police officers are requesting your presence at the scene."

CHAPTER 31

Surprise at Calabasas

July 2–3, 2015

Mike removed a nine-millimeter Sig Sauer semi-automatic handgun and two full mags of ammunition from his father's heavy wall-mounted gun safe. He racked the slide a few times, inserted a full mag into the butt, racked back one more time to place a round in the chamber. There's no safety lever on this weapon. The safety feature is the trigger finger and brain of the user.

Moments later, he released his belt buckle and single button at the top of his fly, allowing the baggy utility pants to fall around his ankles. He stepped away, retrieved a wide, thin elastic belt with a six-inch vertical slit to the right of center, pulled it tight around his hips below the beltline, and engaged the Velcro. He refastened his trousers, held the Sig in his right hand, used his left hand to open the fly, placed two fingers into the slit, stretched the opening out, and slid the weapon inside. A maneuver practiced many times while serving his country. Mike often carried an undeclared weapon into meetings with so-called friendlies.

Well into the forty-five-minute drive to the scene of the killing. *What the hell is going on? This can't be coincidental. There must be a connection to the drug smuggling operation. Why else at my home?* He entered the private drive leading to the ten-acre family estate and saw a security company vehicle and Bruce Briggs standing at the gate. The normally closed gates were standing open.

"Hi, Bruce. I'm sorry about your man's death. Did he have a family?"

"He was a sixty-year-old widower with one adult daughter and two grandchildren. She's taking it hard. They were close. There are no other close relatives. Devon Etheridge was a fine dedicated parent and security officer. We'll all miss him."

"Do you have more details of the incident? I don't understand this thing unless it has some kind of personal connection."

"All we know so far after receiving the alarm. We attempted to make contact with someone in the house by calling your landline. No one answered. Not waiting, our security captain on duty sent the closest available man to investigate and notified the local police. I wasn't aware of it when we last spoke, but our man arrived and made his way around to the rear of the house within seven minutes of receiving the break-in signal. He reported to the captain that a definite break-in had occurred and was waiting outside for backup. It appears that someone had used a heavy landscape stone to destroy all the glass on the west patio."

Mike drove along the asphalt driveway to a circular turnaround near the house and parked the Land Rover behind a sheriff's van and two black unmarked vehicles. A uniformed officer met Mike at the iron gate.

"I'm McGowin officer. What's going on now?"

"Investigator Foshee is waiting for you on the west patio, Mr. McGowin. He'll talk with you there."

Mike continued walking along an old brick path that led around the two-story home to the well-groomed west-side entrance and patio.

Homicide investigator Tony Foshee stepped off the patio.

"Hi, Mike." They shook hands warmly, having met before at community civic functions on several occasions.

Tony said, "Let's start outside where the homicide took place." They walked to a corner of the patio. "The security officer was standing here, well back from the damaged entrance to the house. He was concentrating on the patio point of entry when his attacker approached from behind and stabbed him in the right side of his neck. The knife jab severed the right carotid artery. Another, unnecessary wound was administered as a deep stab wound to the throat just above the breast bone. The puzzling part, the murder weapon was tossed to the ground near the body of the victim."

Mike said, "May I see the knife? Tony, this has some kind of personal connection to me. It may be a message or warning. There's no other reason for this kind of killing."

Entering the house through the open wall, Tony pointed. "That heavy stone was picked up and thrown several times until all six wide panels extending the length of the patio were demolished." He picked up a clear plastic bag containing the knife from a decorative table. "This thing lends itself toward something a man might carry as a personal weapon, maybe a professional."

Mike held the bag for a moment before handing it back. Stunned, he recognized the heavy folding knife as the type taken weeks ago from the late Lance Howell.

"Tony, we need to make ourselves comfortable for a few minutes while I tell you a horrible story relating to a knife similar to this one. But first, was there any additional damage that we should look after?"

"Not that we can find. You may see things different."

"If it isn't evident to you, Tony, then I doubt there'd be anything significant. Let's sit here and go over what I know and what I fear may be going on here. I've been out of the country for the last six weeks. The maid and our other service people are the only ones who should've been on the property during that time. I don't believe any of those people can be connected to this incident. Before I leave here today, I'll provide you with important contact information at FBI Headquarters in Washington, DC. The agent in charge of a recently completed major operation here on the west coast was assistant director Max Findley. I'll advise him or his staff to expect your call. I'm baffled by what's happening now but feel sure that it's connected to recent drug enforcement and FBI arrests here in California. Now, let me tell you what I know."

Mike told the story of another knife, similar to the one held in evidence. He included a short narrative of the drug operation and his own unfortunate participation. Finished with the local investigators, Mike arranged to have armed guards posted around his home on a round-the-clock basis. He looked at his watch and saw it was almost 3:00 AM. Feeling restless and needing time to think through what happened, he entered a service closet from the large kitchen and picked out a particular set of keys. He threw several switches and exited the kitchen into a well-maintained garden near the just-illuminated pool area. He passed one of the armed security guards and checked with him. "Hello, Officer. Anything unusual around this morning?"

"Not that I'm aware of, sir. Can I help you with something?"

"I'm going to be looking over the outlying area and the automobile storage house. Keep an eye on me, please. I may need you."

He left the pool patio and walked down the long lighted path to the vehicle storage area below the swimming pool. He intended to look over the classic cars stored with his mother's Mercedes. *I'm convinced someone familiar with the late Lance Howell and his obsession for revenge has taken over the vendetta. Can't discount the danger to myself or my new family. The events this evening, too personal, stay aware here. Why no mention made of the valuable classic automobiles stored below in the auto warehouse? Had the local police and security patrol failed to inspect this corner of the property following the break-in?* It would be unusual for anyone seeing the auto collection to avoid commenting. Hoped he's wrong.

Mike approached the array of automatic doors with the electronic control on a lanyard around his neck and decided to check out the small entrance doors on each side of the building first. Lightweight doors being a likely entry point for vandals planning to do damage to valuables stored inside. He walked to the left side first. The overhead security light was out. Without hesitating, he turned and walked back toward the pool where the security guard was keeping an eye on him.

Mike explained, "The security light is out over the entrance to the auto storage. It makes my antenna quiver a bit. I'd like for you to palm your weapon, hold it close to your thigh, and walk with me to see what's going on, if anything."

Mike opened his fly, pulled out his weapon, turned, held the weapon close, and walked back down the path. The guard, a short distance away, walked under a small avocado tree on Mike's left and began to approach the darkened door. Both men approached with caution. The guard stared at the darkened door and passed under a larger tree near the parking lot. A dark-clad figure dropped from the tree, knocked him to the hard surface. His handgun skidded away into the dark shadows. Mike remained still, his Sig close to his right leg, ready.

The heavy figure in dark clothing addressed the man on the ground. "Stay down, and you'll live."

Mike elected to stand steady unless the man on the ground was threatened further and stared hard at the attacker. The assailant was ten feet away in poor light. Mike was shocked. Recognition hit him like a falling tree. Lance Howell glared at him through a mask of hate.

"No man ever laid a hand on me and lived! You thought you'd gotten away with it, didn't you? I've lost everything because of your big ass meddling in my business, killed my brother. I want you to know it's now your time. A thousand small cuts, pain won't end until I'm ready."

"I don't know how in hell you arranged this amazing res-urrection, woman beater. It's more than likely short-lived."

Lance attacked, knife in hand. Mike raised the gun, fired twice. Both bullets struck center mass.

Mike saw the soft hollow point projectiles penetrate the dark clothing left of center. He watched the man fall and placed the weapon in his pocket, accessible. He bent down and lifted the injured guard to his feet. Mike looked at the dark-clad figure again and moved into the darkness where the guard's gun had fallen. Certain the assailant was down, he moved his eyes around, looking for the lost weapon.

Lance Howell caught his breath, ran a hand under the bulletproof vest, and massaged his bruised chest. He saw Mike and the guard moving around the darkness. He crawled ten feet to a thick hedge, burrowed himself into the shadow of low hanging limbs, and waited.

Mike looked back. "Son of a bitch has pulled another Houdini act. Quick! Look behind the hedge row while I check the tree. He can't be far away."

The guard returned. "He's not behind the shrubbery. Must be in the tree." He pulled out a small powerful MAG light and directed it into the tree.

Mike reached for the light, directed it into the branches, and walked all around. "The tree is empty. He had a vest on for protection. Be careful. He's full of tricks." He placed the Glock in his belt. "Let's check the hedge again. Direct your light at the shadow along the bottom. I'll take one side. Don't get close enough to the hedge for another attack. Won't be that lucky again."

On his side of the hedge, Mike could see the light shine through the thin growth at the bottom, removing the dark shadow. "Stop!" he yelled. "Move your light back along the bottom again."

Mike pulled his weapon from his belt and backed up several feet. "Come out of the hedge, Lance. The vest won't save you this time."

Lance squirmed out from under the low-hanging branches. He gained one knee, hesitated, ran at Mike, knife pointed at his stomach.

Mike backed away, made two quick headshots, followed up with two more to the groin area. He saw the first soft hollow point lift a section of scalp. The second entered one eye, blowing brain matter out above one ear. "Now, try coming back from that, murdering bastard, just introduced you to the devil."

Investigator Tony Foshee and the bruised-up security guard gathered in Mike's kitchen and watched him brew fresh coffee. "I thought this damn night would never end, Tony."

Mike's call to Washington earlier in the day stimulated action in the local FBI office. Agents familiar with Task Force Able acted at once. They called in representatives from local, state, and federal law enforcement agencies and requested representatives appear at the crime scene for a special briefing. The goal, connect and understand the local killings related to larger ongoing operations. Thus, the noisy crowd assembled earlier in Mike's main dining room. The tiring, noisy meeting was now over.

Bruce Briggs, president of Briggs Security and Investigations, joined Mike and the others in the spacious kitchen.

Mike said, "Thanks for bringing in the two very efficient women on short notice for kitchen service, Bruce. The fresh gee-dunks were the hit of the evening." The women provided several dozen fresh pastries to supplement coffee for the meeting with gathered law enforcement.

Bruce asked, "Did you ever find out who this guy was, Mike?"

"Oh yeah! The FBI has been puzzling over records of Lance Howell and a Larry Howell, both showing the same year of birth. Up to now, the FBI thought they were one and the same person. As it turned out, they were both born in San Bernardino, one year apart and were brothers. As children, they moved to Cabo San Lucas, Mexico, with their mother and did not return to the United States until they were teenagers. Larry had an extensive arrest record and had been running a drug distribution network in the Inland Empire. He seldom traveled to Mexico. The two interacted mainly with Lance in the States."

CHAPTER 32

Even Oceans Come Together

July 3–4, 2015

Mike drove through the parking garage and parked behind the guest house. The place looked quiet. He noticed the small electric harbor boat missing from its customary tie down, then crossed the yard, through the large kitchen, into Barbara Blair's personal office. He found Barbara deeply engrossed in reading from a large cookbook. She looked up.

"You rascal! Stop scaring the dickens out of me. You look tired as hell, Mike. Are you okay?"

"I'm tired, but feel great otherwise. Where is everyone? Much too quiet around here."

"The kids all went to the beach. The ladies wanted to shop at the mall, and your dad took all the men for a harbor cruise. Why don't you take advantage of the quiet and go straight up for a rest? By the way, thanks for the phone call. You relieved everyone's mind."

"Daddy? Wake up. Mom and me, we've been worried about you!"

Mike opened his eyes and squinted into a gorgeous set of blue eyes and very pretty face.

"Hi, sweetie! What time is it?"

"Mom said it's time for you to get up. We've missed you so much."

"Okay. Can I have a hug first?"

Catherine kissed him on the cheek. He pulled her close. Catherine said, "Ouch! Daddy, you need a shave."

He noticed Tracy at the door holding a large cup of coffee. "Do I get a hug too, oh exhausted one?"

"For that big cup of coffee, you get two hugs."

———~·~———

After his last three cups of coffee, Mike said, "Dad, I think I should check into the office right away. I've been away for over a month. That has me worried. How'd the last board meeting go?"

"Don't worry, Mike. Sally and Gayle have everything on track. However, you might want to inspect some of the contractor's work, if you have time. Don't worry about the new projects. We can let those run into next year if we have to. Your most important concerns now? Your new family. All of us here."

"I want Tracy to come with me to my place later. We can be back in time for the gathering at the club tomorrow. I need to check out a few things, and she needs to know what she's getting into. Tracy, what do you think about you and Catherine accompanying me into Los Angeles today? You two can get acquainted with your new home while I drop by the office. Tomorrow I need to visit a couple of job sites before we return here."

Tracy's mom said, "Why don't you leave Catherine here with us so she can get to know Papa Marcus and Barbara?"

"That'd be nice, Mom! What do you think, Mike?"

"Catherine is so much a part of us, Tracy. I don't think we can leave her that long."

"That's too bad, Mike. Mom, that's a great idea. She looked from Mom to Mike. Catherine will enjoy being here with Mom, Papa, and Steph. It'll be much more fun than a long ride into LA. Besides, I have some shopping to do. I'm still wearing borrowed clothing! Is that okay, Mike?"

Everyone laughed at Tracy. Mike hugged her tight. "That does sound good to me."

~~~

Mike drove south with Tracy in the Land Rover and took Highway 101 to Las Vergennes Canyon Road exit. They headed south again until east on Mulholland to a private road. At a huge iron gate, Mike pushed a button on the console. The gates slid open, and they sped through. A large Tudor home stood at the end of the driveway. "What's this, Mike, your country club?" Tracy squeezed Mike's thigh and laughed.

"Mom and Dad built this home, designed the landscaping when I was about Catherine's age. Mom worked as a landscape architect when she met Dad, bid on his projects. She found this ten-acre parcel after their wedding, convinced Dad to work with her building the place."

"Your mother sounds like a very special person, Mike. I want to know everything about her. How did she die, if I may ask?"

"You would've liked her, and she would've loved you. She was always after me to find a girl to settle down with and bring-in grandbabies for her to spoil. Mom died in sort of a freak accident. She liked to ride horses. You'll see the stables later. About five years ago, she purchased a beautiful gelding jumper she loved and rode every single morning. One day while they were out, a coyote jumped out. The horse reared, took off, and ran from under her. Mom fell backward onto the hard-packed bridal trail. She never regained consciousness."

"Oh my god, Mike, how horrible."

"It was tragic for all of us, but I think it caused more serious damage to Dad. He lost interest in the business, sold the horses, and moved to the bay house, as he always called it. Now he just calls it home."

"You must have wonderful memories of growing up here. I can tell it's more than family loyalty. Do you live here all the time, Mike? Or just visit to recharge your energy level?"

"No! It isn't just that. I love this place and hope you and Catherine will love it too. Oh yes, I had a nice apartment on Pico Boulevard before Mom died. But later I realized how important to me this place felt. I couldn't let it become just another piece of property on the market."

"From what I've seen already, Catherine and I would be out of our minds if we objected to living here with you. Finding you and loving you again is all we require. This will be our home, and we'll do our best to make you proud and happy, with maybe just a few minor disappointments from time to time."

She leaned against him, nibbled his ear, and slid a hand along his thigh. Mike stopped and parked in the circular driveway. Tracy's mischievous kisses created havoc with his driving. After a few moments of passion, they left the Land Rover, breathing hard.

Tracy walked to an old-fashioned split rail fence covered with ivy. "Oh my god, Mike! It's beautiful!" She pointed to a fifteen-foot waterfall flowing over black volcanic rock before dropping another two feet into a crystal-clear swimming pool. "The flora and fauna of this place is spectacular. Do I have to clean the pool? Please tell me you have a crew to manage this amazing property!"

Mike laughed. Tracy shifted her attention away from the waterfall. "What's that attractive building with all the big doors there down below the pool cabana?"

They walked in that direction. "That's where we park the cars. The Spanish tile area is for extra parking when entertaining."

Tracy stopped in her tracks. "Will you expect me to do a lot of entertaining?"

"No, honey, trust me. You'll make plenty of friends here. That'll be your call, on your terms. I'll be happy if it's our close friends and family. You and Catherine will have years to choose your friends here."

"Mike, I haven't even been in your gorgeous home. Can we go inside now? What an attractive entrance. The classic leaded glass goes well with the home's overall design. So how does this get managed? Who in the world takes care of it?"

"The pool service is weekly. The gardener comes five days a week. A landscaping company comes semi-monthly, and the maid would like to come in twice each week. At the present time, her crew is here once a week. You can help me evaluate all these services once you're settled and feel at home. You'll be surprised how fast you adjust to managing the estate, which I'll appreciate, so I can concentrate on business. Does it scare you?"

"Not really. In fact, as you explain it, I look forward to sharing the responsibility. I'm overwhelmed at the moment, but most importantly, I want to make you happy and proud of me."

"I'm proud of you, sweetheart, and love you like crazy. It feels like no time at all has passed since we took that plunge into the Christmas tree. Are you sure we haven't been together these last ten years? I've never been so comfortable with anyone else. I always felt we were destined for each other."

"So have I, Mike. I've longed for you, allowed my pride to steal ten years from our lives, and I'm so sorry." Tears welled. They held each other close for a moment, then began moving again through the entrance. He walked her through the house. "I'm overwhelmed with this home, beginning to understand your mother and why you couldn't turn your back on this heritage. It's beautiful, yet unique and personal." They moved into the upstairs rooms. "Every room is large and well furnished with large closets. But why two master bedrooms? Both have floor-to-ceiling glass overlooking the pool area. I'm certain your parents were devoted lovers, not desiring separate bedrooms."

"You're right about that! Until Mom died, this was one large room and very personal. I'll tell you all about it later."

Now in the master bedroom, Tracy wandered near the king-size bed, turned back the covers, and smiled at Mike. "Do you really need to visit your office today, Mike?"

He crossed the room and pulled her close, both hands on her soft backside. "Of course not. I'm going crazy, and I want more than a tender kiss after two weeks so close to the most beautiful girl on the planet."

"I know! I feel the same way. Let's enjoy each other, Mike. The house is beautiful, but we'll appreciate it more if we finish the tour later. I just want to feel you next to me. I'm not ashamed to admit I've dreamed of having you hold me for years. Please, let's take off our clothes. I want to feel you close again."

Mike darkened the room, just enough light left to see each other's eyes. They removed clothing one garment at a time in the soft glow of the recessed lighting, then it wasn't fast enough.

"Do you still love me, Mike? After all this time?"

"So much it hurts. I want many more children with you, maybe even a baker's dozen, honey. Think you can handle it?"

"Hell no! But one more might be nice." Neither can keep their hands off the other. With a hair's distance between the two warm bodies, they continued standing, touching each other with lips and fingertips, bringing intense sensations and deep emotions. Tracy reached for Mike's hand and tugged him to the turned-down bed.

"Hold me, Mike. Hold me so tight it hurts, Mike, please. I want you so much."

Tracy stretched and sat up. "Mike, how long have we been here for gosh sakes? That was a wonderful rediscovery of ourselves, wasn't it? I'm not so sure I can walk to the bathroom, and I still need you close to me, Mike. Please hold me a while longer."

"We now have a lifetime to practice, Tracy. Do you think we need it?" She buried her face against Mike's chest and let tears trickle down her cheek, happy tears. "I'm sorry, Mike. You're the only man who ever made me cry. Even oceans couldn't keep us apart."

CHAPTER 33

The Wrap-Up

July 9, 2015

Max Findley stepped down from the helicopter to the ship's deck. *Whoa, the damn thing's still moving.*

Coast Guard Commander Cheyne Douglas ducked low against the rotor wash, grabbed an elbow, and led Max away from the spinning helicopter rotors. "Welcome aboard US Coast Guard ship Adak, sir. We've been expecting you." He pointed up. "Better watch your head through these low passageways, sir. Agent in charge, Parkhill of DEA, and Homeland Security representative Mr. James Bailey are waiting in the wardroom, Agent Findley."

The wardroom on the Coast Guard ship looked small to him. Agent Parkhill grabbed his hand. "Thank you, Max, for the excellent job you've done getting us to this point. I believe you know Jim Bailey."

"Yes! Hi, Jim. Good to see you."

"Well, gentlemen, things are coming together the way we hoped. Our people on the scene in Mexico sent word this afternoon that Howell's man, Palmyra, made a new delivery at 2:00 PM. Any sooner and we wouldn't have had assets in place for the take down," Parkhill said. He looked right at Max. "You were successful keeping the Catalina Island action out of the news, or we wouldn't be here so soon."

Jim Bailey said, "Yeah, Max, your agents must have laughed their asses off after hearing the rumor coming up from the low-level drug community about Howell's disappearing act. They're saying he took off with his big yacht before cartel discipline caught up with him. Some say he disappeared at the hands of drug lord Federico Quanta."

"Yeah, it's just a matter of time before word filters back to the cartel through Mexican law enforcement," Max said.

Commander Douglas stuck his head in the door. "There's an urgent update for you, Agent Parkhill, from Coast Guard air. The freighter *San Delfino* entered international waters an hour ago. They picked up our vessels on radar, slowed to a crawl."

Parkhill turned to Cheney. "Activate boarding orders at once, Commander. They probably got word about the Port San Quentin raid through Mexican drug enforcement. Let's get those container numbers to the boarding party right away."

Jim Bailey said, "That's damn fast information coming from our agents with the Mexican authorities. A smart move, getting specific container information from arrested crews returning to San Quentin. Must have offered cash incentives and maybe reduced charges."

"Most likely," said Parkhill. "Just the specific information we need. Won't have to open up every damn container on board to get the critical evidence. We also have an update on the raid, gentlemen."

"The operation has proven successful beyond expectations. Already, agents have arrested six major distributors from California, Oregon, and Washington. And listen to this. Thirteen major dealers operating in major cities between the Mexican border and Canadian border have also been apprehended, with more arrests to be made."

Jim Bailey said, "That's great, Chuck. Now let's get the shippers in the net."

Commander Douglas turned from the small computer screen. "Visual aid is now hooked up to the special ops boarding party, gentlemen. Ops personnel rappelled down from helicopters, landed without opposition."

Commander Douglas said, "Container ship *San Delfino* is dead in the water. DEA inspectors are now boarding from small craft. We only have small screen capability here, so gather in close to see what's going on."

Ninety minutes later, James Bailey from Homeland Security turned off his recorder. "That's the damnedest thing I've ever seen. That ship had seven identified containers on board, each carrying at least two small boats loaded with contraband of one kind or another. I congratulate the task force and all of you involved in this well-run operation. Max, it looks like your agents are going to be busy for a while longer running down stragglers."

Jim Bailey sat down at the conference table. "So you and Chuck are heading out to board *San Delfino* for the wrap-up. That should be interesting."

"There's an old saying in the military, Jim, 'No job's done until the paperwork's finished.' The real wrap-up starts then, back in Washington," Max said.

Jim Bailey reached across the table to shake hands. "Thank you, gentlemen, for keeping us informed. Good luck boarding that ship."

The first week of August, Joel Santiago and the Conwell sisters, each in turn, were surprised by a knock at the door. The man flashed his identification. "I'm Agent Stevenson from the Washington office of the Federal Bureau of Investigation. May I see some identification, please?"

Once identified, each person received a sealed envelope marked "PERSONAL" above their name. Federal Bureau of Investigation, Washington, DC, was the return address.

~~~

In late August 2015, Mike McGowin received a short text message from Max Findley. "The Eagle has delivered. You owe me."

PAINTING BY
CHUCK ESTVAN

Jerry Baggett is a long time Los Angeles businessman and South California yachtsman. Jerry grew up on Cape Hatteras Island and the Gulf Coast of Alabama where he developed a love for the sea. After graduating from the University of Alabama in 1958, he soon found his way to Los Angeles where he has spent the last forty years splitting his time between his various business interests and his love for cruising and diving the ever-fascinating barrier islands of Southern California with his family. Jerry has been a member of the Pacific Corinthian Yacht Club in Channel Island Harbor for many years. This is his first book.

CPSIA information can be obtained
at www.ICGtesting.com
Printed in the USA
FSOW03n0917211117
41483FS